G000143861

Paul D. Brazill's books include *Small Time Crimes, Guns Of Brixton, The Last Laugh, A Case Of Noir, Big City Blues* and *Kill Me Quick!* He was born in England and lives in Poland. His writing has been translated into Italian, Finnish, Polish, German and Slovene. He has been published in various magazines and anthologies, including *The Mammoth Book of Best British Crime*.

Also by Paul D. Brazill

SMALL TIME CRIMES
LAST YEAR'S MAN
GUNS OF BRIXTON
THE LAST LAUGH
A CASE OF NOIR
BIG CITY BLUES
TOO MANY CROOKS
KILL ME QUICK

Gumshoe Blues

The Peter Ord Yarns

Paul D Brazill

Close To The Bone
An imprint of Gritfiction Ltd

Contents

Gumshoe Blues

In the beginning was the sound. The light came later. The sound was a horrifying wail that skewered its way deep into my unconscious brain, until I awoke swiftly, sharply - drowning in sweat, my heart smashing through my ribcage; my head about to burst. Some twat, somewhere, was playing a U2 song, over and over again, and all was far from friggin' quiet on New Year's Day.

I forced my eyes open and squinted until I saw the familiar sight of a fraying Seatown United poster peeling from fuzzy, red-flock wallpaper. I was lying on a brown tweed sofa and tangled up in a tartan blanket that had seen better days and nights. I was home.

The air in the room was warm and soupy, and I felt a wave of nausea pass over me. I closed my eyes, took a deep breath and counted to ten. The dry heaves kicked in around six. A beat. I peeled my eyes open again. The aquarium bubbled and gurgled, bathing the room in a sickly green light. Sickly and yet soothing. I reminded myself that I really had to put some tropical fish in there one day.

I edged onto my side and awkwardly kicked the blanket to the floor. I was fully clothed. My armpits were soaking. My fake Armani shirt was soggy. A sickly smell permeated my pores and the least said about my trousers the better.

Beside me was a sticky coffee table that was cluttered with the remnants of the previous night's drinking session. I picked up an open can of Stella Artois and shook it. It was more than half full. A result, then.

I slowly sipped the beer can's warm, flat contents until I started to get a glow on, like one of the kids in the old Ready-Brek adverts. Booze: central heating for piss-heads.

Bonzo, The Ledge, and their musically illiterate pals continued to strangle a cat in the flat next door, and I knew that I was going to have to make a move soon, before my head went all *Scanners*. I finished the lager, edged myself up to a sitting position, and picked up my glasses from the coffee table. One of the lenses was scratched, but at least they weren't broken. Another result.

The blinking, digital clock-radio that was plonked on top of the television set, said that it was 3.15am. It was always 3.15am, ever since I'd thrown it against the wall during a particularly grating late night phone-in show. In the real dark night of the soul, there was always some twat talking bollocks at three o'clock in the morning.

I grabbed my knock-off Armani jacket from the floor and fumbled in the pockets for my mobile phone. It was just after ten. That gave me enough time to get ready and make myself presentable before my midday meeting with Jack Martin.

My stiff joints ached as I shuffled towards the kitchen, and I noticed that my shoes were stained with something that looked a lot like blood, but was much more likely to be chilli sauce from the doner kebab I vaguely remembered stuffing down my gob the night before.

I put on the kettle and crushed a couple of diazepam and codeine into an Xmas turkey-flavour 'Pot Noodle': most important meal of the day. My headache was starting to settle into a steady throb, but my throat was like a nun's knickers. I foolishly opened the buzzing fridge to look for a cold beer, but the smell made my stomach lurch and the waves of nausea quickly built to a tsunami.

I staggered toward the toilet bowl and evacuated my New Year's Eve overindulgence. After a minute or two of retching, I kneeled on the linoleum, whimpering and panting like a stray dog.

Wiping my mouth on the back of my hand, I went back to the living room and poured myself a large vodka and orange.

Happy New Year.

Out with the old and in with the new.

***

Truth be told, my most vivid and powerful memories of

childhood were always in black and white. The monochrome Saturday morning *Kidz Klub* serials that were shown at the local Odeon cinema, and the Hollywood films on afternoon television, when I was throwing a sickie from school. It all seemed so much more vibrant than anything that real life could come up with. And, as you would expect of someone who grew up living more fully in his imagination than in the day-to-day, adulthood proved to be a series of disappointments and non-events.

Nightclubs, for example, were, in my mind, bustling with tough guys in pinstriped suits, wise-cracking cigarettes girls and sultry femme fatales belting out torch songs on a Chiaroscuro-lit stage. So, when I eventually stumbled into the grim reality – claggy carpets, overflowing toilets, beer-bellied men staggering around a dance floor with leathery, bottle blondes: well, my heart sank like the Titanic.

Not that Velvettes was a nightclub, of course. Not as such. It was supposed to be an exclusive 'Gentleman's Club' close to the Marina's yuppie flats. In other words, it was an up-market strip joint. Since it was New Year's Day, Velvettes wasn't open to the public and it looked pretty bloody garish in the cold light of day – all shiny chrome and red and black leather. It was like something out of *American Psycho* or an eighties porno film-set. The kitsch theme continued with a stained-glass recreation of the famed poster of a female tennis player scratching her arse that many a teenage boy had on their wall in the Seventies. I'd even splashed out on one myself.

"It's not exactly Sophie's Choice, is it?" I said, fiddling with a sticky beer mat. "It's just a hypothetical question."

"Naw, it's a wotsit," said Tuc, Velvettes' behemoth of a barman, running his fingers through his close-cropped hair. "It's entrapment." His East London accent stumbled further forward with every sip of Stella, not that he'd ever really lost it completely. I had no idea what had dragged Tuc from his life down The Smoke to Seatown, this fading one-whore-town on the north east coast of England. And, to be honest, I thought it was for the best not to ask. There were rumours that he was the bastard offspring of the dead billionaire Robert Maxwell and although I didn't know anything about that, whatever he was, he was certainly one sort of a bastard. A hard bastard.

In fact, Tuc was so hard that one of his regular party pieces was to see how many times he could head-butt a rabbit, using the small crucifix that was tattooed on his forehead as his 'sight.' Although, he gave up that little pastime, along with quite a few others that were equally as unsavoury, when he met Wendy.

As part of an ASBO, Tuc had been forced to attend regular 'addiction awareness sessions' at the ever-popular Albion Road Substance Abuse Centre – or ARSESUCK , as it was more commonly known – in order to help him 'deal with his self-medication issues'. The effectiveness of these sessions could be judged by the anthill of happy talc he'd just vacuumed up his nostrils in two seconds flat. But, while he was there he'd first encountered Wendy Hope, the last of the flower children, who quite miraculously transformed him into a tree-hugging vegetarian and introduced him to the dubious delights of all manner of New Age and self-help carryings-on, including acupuncture sessions to help with his various cravings.

Indeed, as we spoke, Tuc was fiddling with the clusters of multi-coloured acupuncture needles that pierced his ears. He had so many now that he was starting to look like the bloke from the *Hellraiser* films.

I sipped my half-pint of Kronenbourg and looked longingly at the constellation of booze bottles that were glimmering below the bar's flickering Jack Daniels sign, tempting me like a row of hookers in a high-class bordello.

"And, anyway, I ain't no shirt-lifter, am I?" Tuc continued, scratching his tattooed neck.

"I'm not saying that you're gay, Tuc, but, if, for some reason, you did have to, you know, make the two-backed beast with another bloke, what would you do? Is it better to give than to receive?"

I couldn't resist it, even though messing with Tuc's mind was like shooting fish in a barrel. He wasn't the sharpest tool in the box, after all. He'd received his nickname after the time he'd tattooed a dotted line and the word 'cut' around his neck, while looking in a mirror.

"I'm saying nothing," he said, and he struck a match on the NO SMOKING sign behind the bar. Some wag had used a marker pen and changed it to NO SUCKING.

Tuc lit up with a sulky look on his face and turned to the CD player. "Fancy a bit of Barry Shite?" he said.

"Aye, why not," I said.

Tuc walked over to a massive sound system and picked up a remote control. As the *Love Unlimited Orchestra* kicked in, I looked at my reflection in the mirror behind the bar and was pleased to see that the effects of the hangover were only internal. All I saw was a common-or-garden, bespectacled, middle-aged man in a well-cut suit. A chief accountant, maybe, or a solicitor, but certainly not a Private Investigator. And that was just how I liked it: really. Easier to be *incognito*. If I ever got a proper case.

"So, what does the gaffer want?" said Tuc. "I've never known him use a private eye before. He's got plenty of his own geezers, if he needs anything hush-hush."

I shrugged.

"Haven't got a clue. I thought you'd know," I said.

"Mr Martin ain't said a dicky bird to me," said Tuc.

There was a grumbling in my stomach, like a tank rolling down Tiananmen Square. It was either the Ginsters sausage roll I'd bought from a petrol station on the way over to Velvettes, or a sense of trepidation.

A red light bulb that dangled over the bar flashed.

"Well, now's your time to find out," said Tuc.

He nodded toward a crimson cushioned door at the end of the bar. "Off you trot."

I pushed the door open and immediately heard *The Archers* theme.

Jack Martin, the owner of Velvettes, and a string of other strip joints in the region, sat in a red leather armchair. He was in his late sixties. He had salt-and-pepper hair that erred on the side of Saxa, and his face had that scrubbed-by-a-Brillo-Pad look favoured by football managers like Sir Alex Ferguson. As I walked into the red leather-and-oak office, Jack was scrutinising the *Sunday Times* crossword through half-moon glasses.

"One across, five letters. Question: To egg on. Answer: Toast," I said.

"Yes, very sharp," said Jack, gesturing at me to sit down. "You'll be cutting yourself, if you're not too careful." Despite his Newcastle accent, his nicotine-stained and brandy-brimmed voice still sounded more than a little like the tiger from Disney's The Jungle Book cartoon.

"What can I do you for, Mr M?" I said.

Jack Martin put down his paper and examined my business card. "Peter Ord, Private Investigator," he said. "Very... stylish looking card."

I'd got my niece, Kaylee, an art-student, to work on the card's design. The loop of the P had been made into a deerstalker hat and O had been drawn to look like the lens of a magnifying glass. It had seemed like a good idea at the time.

"Do you mind if I ask you a personal question?" he said.

"Fire away."

"Were you a big fan of Mrs Thatcher's stint as Prime Minister, Peter?" said Jack.

"Not too bothered either way," I answered. "I'm not exactly what you'd call a particularly political animal."

"Head in the clouds, head in the sand, eh?" said Jack, with a look of distaste. He plonked a bottle of expensive looking brandy on his desk along with two glasses.

"Cheers," said Jack, filling both glasses. He pushed one towards me.

"Cheers," I said.

"You see, Mrs T was, in many ways, a visionary, Peter. She believed in an aspirational society," said Jack. "Get on your bike; go for it; seize the day; grab the bull by the horns. That sort of thing."

I sipped my brandy, enjoying the burn.

"But, that's not for everyone, is it? Ninety-nine per cent of the population are just here to make up the numbers. Cannon fodder. They live on dreams. Hopes. They live their shitty little lives and week after week they wait for their lottery numbers to come up, hoping for a way out of the mire. They spend their winnings in their mind just before the numbers are drawn and then drown their sorrows in watered down lager and strong cider when they don't win the jackpot. Hope is the real opium of the masses, Peter."

He knocked back his drink and poured himself another one. "And this is where I and my little dream factories come in. The punters shuffle into my clubs and catch an eyeful of the dancers; Brazilian, Thai, Ukrainian. As exotic as you like. And they look at them and think:

Wouldn't crawl over that to get to the wife. And of course, these girls see this. They see the most desperate. And they flirt with them and the suckers just eat it up. So, when the dancers invite them into one of the booths for a private dance, well, of course your customer says yes. Hoping for a bit of hanky-panky, or at least a hand shandy"

I finished my drink and Jack refilled my glass.

"And we make a packet out of them because, although they never get so much as a sniff, they keep coming back. As I said, people live in hope."

He sat on the edge of the desk.

"So, it would not be conducive to good business practice if I let one or two of these ladies actually give the customer a little too much satisfaction, would it?"

"I suppose not."

"And, indeed, it would be in my interest to find out which, if any of them, was actually doing this. Which is why I'm hiring you, of course."

I nodded.

"Here's the deal. I want you to frequent Velvettes and some of my other clubs, from time to time, to see if you get offered... a bit of touch and go, or even a full service, from one of the girls. Or see one of them arranging a dangerous liaison with a customer... or even a member of staff. Fraternising is not allowed on my premises. Understand?"

And of course I understood. Everything was crystal clear. Jack Martin was hiring me because I looked like a desperate, sex-starved loser. The sort of bloke, in fact, that any resourceful, gold-digging stripper would recognise as ripe for the fleecing.

Flattery will get you everywhere.

***

The first weekend of the New Year was like being stuck in a run-down border town, situated somewhere between disappointment and false hope. Consequently, Velvettes was so crowded it was suffocating. The place was stuffed with sweaty, shifty-looking middle-aged men, and half-naked women wandering around with pint glasses full of money. An overweight DJ wearing a pink court jester's hat played back-to-back hits of the 80s. On the tiny stage a tall, statuesque blond, naked except for a pair of angel's wings strapped to her back, canoodled with a glistening silver pole as Dexy's Midnight Runners invited us to *Come On Eileen*.

I was standing at the bar finishing a packet of dry-roasted peanuts when someone tapped me on the shoulder.

"Private dance?" said a petite South American girl with a sticky accent. She was dressed in a red nylon nurse's uniform that crackled when she moved. Her lipstick was crimson, her fingernails, the same colour. And so was my face.

"Aye," I said and followed her to the back of the room and into what looked like a darkened priest's confession box. She clicked the door closed and red light filled the room, which was more than a little cramped. Not enough room to swing a dick.

"Please sit," she said.

I plonked myself down in a leather armchair and grinned.

"I'm Maria," she said. "Come here often?"

"Innuendo and out the other, eh?" I replied, with an anxious smirk. "I thought innuendo was a gay bar in Milan, eh?"

I was babbling, nervously.

Maria looked confused.

"Sorry, I don't understand," she said.

I coughed.

"I don't come here as much as I'd like to," I said.

She smiled.

The instrumental version of ABC's *The Look Of Love* played as she started an air dance – no touching, no grinding herself into my lap – just the odd moment when her hand or knee accidentally brushed my skin.

Cue: goose bumps; a lump in the throat and a lump elsewhere. And it was easy to see how it worked. How a punter could think: maybe she meant to touch me. Maybe she fancies me. Maybe, baby, I don't know. It was the old brain/body dichotomy in action.

Jack Martin was right about people living in hope.

***

"How long were you married, Ordy?" asked Tuc, as I leaned on the corner of the bar and flicked through my divorce papers. I'd actually received them a couple of days before, but had only just plucked up the courage to read them.

"Fourteen years," I said. "I don't remember breaking two friggin' mirrors, though."

Tuc nodded sagely, as I stuffed the documents into my jacket pocket.

Angie Beale and I had been joined at the waist for just over thirteen years before the cracks started appearing in what, I'd thought, was a fairly solid relationship, despite its sporadically psychotic episodes – episodes which were invariable exacerbated by the copious amounts of alcohol we imbibed. The foundations of the house of love had started to shake, however, with the reappearance of a positively seismic blast from Angie's past – her erstwhile fiancé Greg Bardsley, an overweight local councillor with an equally corpulent bank account. And so, one wet and windy night in May, after a particularly prolific drinking session, I challenged Greg to what I suppose once upon a time would have been referred to as a duel. We both ended up in a dark and dingy alley outside the Methodist church, stripped to the waist in the pouring rain, illuminated by the light from a stained-glass window. Greg had bopped around like Mohammad Ali, albeit a fat, white and wheezy Mohammed Ali, as I took off my jacket, shirt and horn-rimmed glasses and carefully placed them on a wheelie bin for safekeeping. As I turned around I was sucker-punched by a big pink blancmange that sent me hurtling into a pile of black bin bags.

"And let that be a lesson to you," I said to Greg who was towering over me like a gloating Godzilla over a demolished Tokyo.

"Wanker," he replied, before triumphantly waddling off hand in glove with Angie, leaving me to light a cigarette, lie back, close my eyes, and inhale deeply in a manner that I hoped was reminiscent of Jean-Paul Belmondo at the close of Jean-Luc Godard's À Bout de Souffle.

The following day I decided to quit my job and become a Private Eye. Some people put it down to the bang on the head.

"Penny for your thoughts," said Tuc.

"Can I keep the change?" I said, and carried on drinking.

The late evening segued into the early hours of the morning. The crowd at Velvettes was thinning out. As the dancers hovered around the bar there was a cacophony of foreign accents. It was a nice sound, too. A refreshing change.

Seatown was your archetypal claustrophobic small town. It was tucked away on the north east coast of

England and its awkward location meant that you couldn't really end up here by accident. All the main roads and motorways bypassed the place. People rarely moved from the town, and not too many outsiders decided to settle here either.

I was swimming in self-pity and brandy. Mostly brandy. Tuc poured me another drink, as Maria wandered over. She was dressed in a black sweater and jeans, and carrying a Marks & Spencer's carrier bag.

"Have you finished your shift?" I said.

"Ah, the great detective," she said. 'I have finished for the night, yes.'

"Can I buy you a drink?"

I could feel Tuc's laser beam gaze, knowing that I really shouldn't have been 'fraternising' with the performers.

"Of course," said Maria. "Tequila!"

"Tequila for the lady," I slurred.

I winked at Tuc, finished my brandy and headed toward oblivion like dirty dishwater down a plughole.

The next morning, the sound of the doorbell dragged me by my lapels out of the abyss and into consciousness. The day was migraine bright and I woke up with a sense of dread that was even worse than usual. When I saw Maria sleeping next to me I knew why.

The doorbell wouldn't stop ringing. It was like a stiletto grinding through my brain. It was even worse than a U2 song. I sat up.

"What is it?" said Maria, sitting upright, exposing her bought and paid-for breasts.

"Dunno," I said, my voice cracking. "I'd best have a gander."

I reached over to the bedside table, picked up a box of Tic Tacs and Poured them carefully into my mouth.

Crunching the mints, I slowly got up, pulled on a pair of jeans and stumbled toward the door hoping, just this once, that it was a Jehovah's Witness. Furtively, I peeked through the letterbox and was pretty damned sure it wasn't. And I doubted that it was the Avon Lady, either, unless she had a tattoo around her neck. I looked over at Maria and crawled back into the bed. I was so far up shit creak an outboard motor wouldn't help, let alone a paddle, so why not go out with a bang instead of a whimper.

***

When I decided to become a Private Investigator, although I certainly didn't have any romantic illusions that the profession would bear much of a resemblance to the lives of Marlowe and Spade, I had, at least, a smattering of hope that there might be a little silver screen glamour to the job. Over the years, however, that hope and I, had barely been on nodding terms. So it wasn't the greatest of shocks to find out that I'd have to take on sideline jobs here and there. Being a store detective, for example, seemed a fairly reasonable 'sideways career shift'. Even working as a security guard wasn't that much of a stretch. But not being Santa Claus. In *Poundland*. Ahem.

And, with Christmas over and done with, I'd lost even that job. I was skint and desperately in need of some work. And desperate times called for desperate measures.

"*Poundland*'s next to Poundworld, across the road from All 4 A Pound, mate," I said to Bryn Laden, who was clearly taking great pleasure in my humiliation.

"Near *Greggs*, then?" he said. He stretched his arms out wide as he yawned.

There were sweat patches under the arms of his raincoat. Quite an accomplishment, that.

"There are more Greggs in this town than there are cockneys at a Man United game, Bryn. Everywhere's near Greggs," I said.

I looked out of Keith & Babs Key-Babs' window as snowflakes started to fall like confetti. A motorcade of buggies stuffed with chubby kids and pushed by chubbier women rolled past and up the ramp toward the granite-grey delights of Seatown Shopping Centre, the personification of Seventies architecture and rumoured soon to become a listed building. Shit, then.

"YTS shoplifters," said Bryn, pointing a shaky finger at one of the kids.

I nodded and smiled. Oscar Wilde once said that only a fool didn't judge by appearances and if you asked anyone to describe their idea of what a sleazy hack looked like then Bryn Laden would surely fit the bill perfectly; lank hair, hanging down like rats' tails, red nose, waxy raincoat and, of course, permanently pissed.

Bryn had always dreamed of becoming a writer, mind you, even when we were at school. As soon as he hit sixteen, he left the comp and got a job as an apprentice at the Seatown Gazette. He stayed there for a while, picked up what he could – including the owner's wife – and then headed off down south, like a tiddly Dick Whittington, to seek his fortune. And he almost found it, too.

He'd worked on a now-defunct Sunday tabloid for many years, doing all manner of jobs – horse racing correspondent, horoscope writer, celebrity interviewer, television columnist – but after the rag in question went under because of hacking a much-loved celebrity's mobile phone, he headed back to Seatown.

It wasn't exactly a hail-the-conquering-hero welcome, either. His former employer's infamous reputation closed more doors than it opened, that was for sure.

These days, his main income was from finding the most sleazy and least salubrious stories in the Eastern European tabloids, translating them via Google and selling them to the red tops, who were always keen to point an outraged finger at the goings-on of Johnny and Jenny Foreigner.

It was early evening and we were the kebab shop's only customers. Even Keith had gone to the flat above the shop to watch *Buffy The Vampire Slayer*, and Babs, as per usual, had turned toward Mecca – she went to the bingo eight days out of seven. We were sitting at a small red Formica table, in front of a massive mural of the New York skyline at night. Bryn was taking sips from a miniature bottle of *Grouse* and sweating like Jimmy Savile in a morgue. A plasma television showed back-to-back Polish speedway races.

"Computers, Ordy," he said as he threw the red cabbage from his kebab into a waste paper bin that was overflowing with the stuff. "Big Daddy is watching you."

He pointed to the CCTV above the door. "Piece of piss to find anyone these days."

Bryn took an old betting slip from the bin and wrote a name and number on it. Handed it to me. "Are you still on the wagon?" he said.

"That was a short-lived caprice," I said. "If I don't get a decently paid job soon, though, I'll be throwing myself under a wagon."

"Or your landlord will do the job for you."

Bryn chuckled to himself, but knowing Carl 'Rachman' Raymond, it wasn't that unlikely a prospect. Carl's anger management issues were well known. One of his tenants had apparently tried to hide from him in a pizza oven and when Carl found him he just turned the oven on and went outside for a ciggy.

Bryn handed me the bottle of *Grouse*. I took a swig.

"I thought Jack Martin had some work for you?" said Bryn.

I squirmed in my seat.

"Yes, well, unfortunately, that one went a little, er, pear-shaped, as they used to say on *The Bill*."

I was, in fact, keeping as far away from Jack Martin, and Tuc, as possible, until things cooled down.

Bryn tapped the betting slip in my hand. "That should sort you out," he said. "Decent dosh, and it should get you out and about for a bit."

"Yeah, don't think I don't appreciate it, Bryn. But, you know, the thought of working for him is giving me worse indigestion than Mucky Mary's curry and chips."

"Needs must," said Bryn.

And he was right.

He threw the rest of his kebab in the bin and we headed out into a cold January night. Seatown High Street was pretty much deserted and I noticed that, once again, someone had stolen the 'U' from the *Poundland* sign. I resisted the temptation to buy a tin of spray paint and write 'Pondland – Shops for Pondlife' across its metal shutters but it was a struggle.

I took out my Nokia and dialled the number on the betting slip that Bryn had given me. My prospective client answered.

"It's Peter Ord," I said.

He chuckled and gave me an address.

"Aye," I said. "I know the place."

I hung up.

"Action stations?" said Bryn

"Aye," I said.

"Where and when are you meeting him?"

"At the windmill. In half an hour," I said. "But I think I need some reinforcements, before I go up there."

We crossed the street towards a symbol of the faded local gentry that was, without irony, known as The Grand Hotel.

"Craig Ferry?" said Bryn, as if he were having a tooth pulled.

"Why not?" I said. "He owes me."

"Yeah, but he could talk a glass eye to sleep."

As we walked up the hotel's steps, I had a memory of Craig and I burying a dead kangaroo in a freezing cold, rain-soaked graveyard. Yes, Craig Ferry owed me big time.

The Grand Hotel, like a fair amount of its clientele, was all fur coat and no knickers. It had actually lived up to its name once upon a time and its façade was still pretty impressive, but the interior left a lot to be desired. For many years, it had survived as a nightclub which was just about bog standard, with the emphasis on the bog.

Every Thursday was 'Super Seventies Special' night because, unsurprisingly, the music that was played was from the 70s and all the drinks were 70p.

In fact, most of the clientele were knocking on seventy, too, which is why it had earned its reputation as a grab-a-granny night. And why it suited my quarry, Craig Ferry, down to the ground.

The Ferry family were fairly successful villains on their way to becoming respectable. Craig was the youngest of the four Ferry boys, and he'd been born premature and weak, leading his mother to become a tad overprotective of him. For most of his childhood he hardly left her side and he had, it seemed, developed a bit of an Oedipus complex. Hence his regular attendance at the 'Super Seventies Special'.

Craig had been a sickly child, as I said, but when he

reached sixteen and his mother died, he transformed himself in a manner akin to that of Bruce Banner turning into *The Incredible Hulk*, albeit at a decidedly slower rate.

When he was a kid, Craig was almost anorexic, but with his mother off the scene, he soon became a fast food and beer-consuming monster. And that, combined with his scoffing of steroids and frequent trips to the gym, spawned the suntanned (a suntan so bright I considered looking for sunglasses) behemoth that was standing at the end of the bar gargling cider and blackcurrant and singing along to Sparks' *This Town Ain't Big Enough For The Both Of Us*.

"It's like the cast of *Cocoon* here," said Bryn as we walked in. "I feel like the kid in that Bruce Willis film. I see dead people."

"They play some tasty tunes, though," I said.

"Gladys Shite and The Pimps, eh?" said Bryn, as *Midnight Train To Georgia* crept out of the tiny sound system.

The place was half empty. There were a few familiar faces but none of them were under sixty-five.

A gangling scarecrow stood at the fruit machine, pumping in coins. Paddy Johnston. Paddy's face was like a blackcurrant crumble and so lived-in that squatters wouldn't stay there. He was wearing his beer-stained Concorde Security Services uniform, head wobbling around like one of those little toy dogs that people used to have in the back of their cars in the sixties, and fiddling with an unlit Embassy cigarette.

"How's things Paddy?" I said.

"What do you think?" he said, jabbing a finger to emphasize the words, as if he were playing darts with them. "Working? Aren't I. On my birthday, eh?"

I just shrugged in an exaggerated way. Paddy had more birthdays than the Queen. I headed towards the bar before he tried to cadge another drink from me.

Craig spotted me and stumbled over.

"Ordy!" he bawled, like a cross between a coked-up Brian Blessed and a deaf lumberjack. "On the lash or on the tap?"

He nodded over to the cast of The Golden Girls who were doing a conga around the room.

"Neither," I said. "I've got a business meeting in unfriendly territory and I need some back up."

"So this is the pint of no return, then," said Craig, and downed the rest of his Strongbow cider in one.

We walked outside and flagged down one of Seatown's New York-style yellow cabs. It stuttered to a halt in front of us. I was taken aback for a moment when I saw that the driver was wearing sunglasses and then I realized it was Roy Ormesby the best known but least popular of the town's Roy Orbison tribute acts.

"Morning, Roy," I said.

"Eh?" he said, went to take his glasses off, then stopped.

"Cunny funt," he said, in that weird transatlantic accent of his.

The three of us just about managed to jam ourselves into the back seat, with me in the middle. The Big O's, *Wild Hearts Run Out Of Time*, played at a low volume through raspy speakers.

"This is cozy," said Bryn.

"Where to?" hissed Roy.

I told him and he looked at us disapprovingly before kissing the statue of the Virgin Mary on his dashboard.

A cracking sound came from somewhere under the car and the deodorant-soaked taxi set off. It shuddered along the high street, past the usual run down pubs, greasy spoons, gift shops, and amusement arcades, and headed out of town.

There were loads of road-works as ever, so Roy took the car along the sea front. Out at sea, a fishing trawler adorned with Christmas lights bobbed up and down on the waves.

The taxi stopped at a set of traffic lights. Outside, I could hear the heavy bass of an old Public Image song and watched a familiar face get off the number six bus. Tuc was heading to his monthly AA meeting.

It was one of those 'bendy' buses that had sprung up recently. I'd had to endure what seemed like about a hundred people subjecting me to the same crap joke as to how the concertina part of the bus should have played a tune when it turned the corner.

Tuc lit up as he crossed the street. The AA meetings were held at the same place every week – the old Wesley Church near the greyhound track – and there was a handful of shifty looking characters hanging around outside smoking cigarettes. I watched as Tuc walked up and joined them.

A few of the faces were familiar – Carole Anders, my old English teacher, was one of them. She sported a brown eye-patch as the result of a drunken brawl with one of the sixth formers she taught. I'd seen it reported in the local paper.

She waved at Tuc and went back to whispering to a gangling, bookish type who wore glasses that were at least as strong as the Hubble Telescope: Fast Eddy.

"Did you hear about Eddy?" said Bryn.

"I've heard a lot about Fast Eddy, none of it good," I said.

I'd known Eddy for donkey's years. From back in the days when I was a teacher and he was the school bus driver. The slowest, most overly cautious driver you could ever meet. Hence the nickname.

"Not heard about his latest romantic escapade, then?"

"Dunno," I said. "I lose track. Do tell."

"Well, they say he met some young lass on the Internet. ShitFacedbook or something. Was getting on really well with her too, until he made the fatal error of sending her his picture that is, and then she blocked him."

I could understand the girl's consternation. Eddy was once described as being like an uglier version of Shane McGowan. Without the charm.

"And what happened?" I said, almost interested.

"Well, he had an idea of where she lived. Some hick village in Scotland. And so he started to spend every weekend going up there on the train and walking around the place looking for her. Until he got picked up by the police for being drunk and disorderly, that is. Thing is, though, it turned out that he'd got the wrong village anyway!"

Bryn gave a cruel cackle.

"Sounds typical of Eddy's luck with women," I said.

"Aye and the trouble is, he's shit with cards, too."

The cab headed up Raby Hill until it came to a full stop outside a converted windmill that loomed over the town like a great black bat. A blinking neon sign hung above the oak front door.

Harry Shand's Bar.

There was a time when Seatown had even more of an American theme going on than just its yellow taxi cabs. Once upon a time, almost half of the bars and nightclubs in the town had been given names like 42nd Street, Times Square, Madison Avenue, Liberties and, unfortunately, The Bowery. There was even a greasy spoon called Hell's Kitchen.

They were all owned by Jordan Rivers, who was more commonly known as Captain Cutlass. Cutlass was a sea coal baron, which meant he regularly employed a motley crew to drive jeeps up and down the beach at low tide and dig up the coal. They then sold it door to door, back in the days when people had coal fires. He'd made a packet, too.

After he'd gotten into the sea coal game, Cutlass also made a mint smuggling booze and cigarettes into the docks. He used to stand at the front of the boats waving a massive sword about. Hence the nickname, although I do believe the sword was actually a rapier.

Indeed, Captain Cutlass was in the process of buying up all the slaver-palaces in Seatown until he mysteriously disappeared on a trip around the local brewery. His body was apparently found two days later, stuffed head-first into a beer barrel. There were worse ways to die.

So his properties were up for grabs and Harry Shand was pretty sharpish with the grabbing.

Harry Shand's Bar was a smoky, pokey dive that had started to earn itself the nickname The Speakeasy although I suspect The Shithole may have been a more accurate description of the place.

However, like some Prohibition-era gin joint, The Speakeasy was a place where businessmen and working girls, cops and robbers, actors and agents and all manner of assorted waifs and strays rubbed shoulders without getting each other's backs up.

Tonight, as usual, the place was littered with the cream of Seatown's flotsam and jetsam. My ex-wife's husband-to-be, Councillor Greg Bardsley, sat at the bar arguing about football with Shand and an unshaven, long haired comedian that I'd occasionally seen on local television. Bardsley was now the owner of two successful bakery chains that had spread across the north-eastern region like the clap – The Man With The Flan and The Gateaux Superstar.

My stomach rolled as I spotted the gangster twins Ronnie and Roger Kruger sitting in a darkened corner of the room with a couple of their no-necked cronies.

The fading club singer Jimmy Golden was fast asleep and drooling on Ronnie Kruger's shoulder, and the disgraced boxer and fence Henry Costa was playing cards with Detective Inspector Sandal, a copper who was so bent you could use him as a pipe cleaner. It was a classy joint alright.

"Well, if it isn't Peter Ord, the private dickhead," said Ronnie Kruger. His stooges burst into uproarious laughter. "Top dollar act this one, lads. A real Tom Selleck. Doesn't even have an office and lives above a clapped-out amusement arcade, you know," said Roger. Their chuckles sounded like Kalashnikovs.

"I'll be wanting a word with you soon enough, Ord," said Roger, which wasn't exactly a piece of information that I wanted to hear.

After my dad was made redundant from his job at the lighthouse, debt was always hanging over my family. One of my earliest memories was of going to Raymond Kruger's pawn brokers, a dark and dingy shop that you entered from a cobblestoned back street so as to avoid the shame of being seen going in. And I clearly remember regularly sticking my skinny kid's fingers into the back of the television's ten bob meter to snaffle enough coins to put the gas or electric on. Or searching down the back of sofa for Embassy cigarette coupons to take to the corner shop and exchange for chopped pork for sandwiches. And when the rent man cometh, he didn't always get paid.

Whenever I saw the Krugers, I always had an unwelcome flashback to those times.

Despite being identical twins, Ronnie and Roger looked little like each other these days. Roger was slim and kept himself super fit. His hair was long and as black as ink. Ronnie, on the other hand, was going bald and more than a little podgy, his predilection for fry ups being mainly responsible for his physique. And he was also mental. Barking, and I don't mean the town in Essex. It was rumoured that he went to bed with a teddy bear and a machete. One thing the Kruger Twins did share, though, was a violent temper.

I just nodded and smiled. Jimmy Golden opened a bleary eye, burped, and knocked back a shot of gin, before going back to sleep.

My footsteps echoed on the cold concrete floor as I walked up to the bar and nodded at Councillor Bardsley.

"Evening Bread Van," I said.

Bardsley cringed as he heard his old school nickname.

Greg Bardsley hadn't always been known as Bread Van, of course. Like most fat kids with glasses of that era, he'd been nicknamed Billy Bunter for most of his childhood.

But when he was eleven, on his first day at Comprehensive School, he earned a new nickname that stuck to him for most of his life.

Spruced up in his new uniform, Greg had stood on the corner near Palmers Bakery, waved goodbye to his mother, and crossed the road toward the school gates.

Within seconds he was knocked over by a bakery delivery van. He was rushed to hospital pretty damn quickly and was off school for the whole term.

The following year, first day of term, same corner,

same van, same driver, the same thing happened again. Blam, as they say.

After that he was never at school. His mother ended up getting a wad of compensation from the bakery, apparently, and paid for him to have private lessons at home. But, someone along the way dubbed him Bread Van and the nickname stuck for quite a while.

Oh, and when he left school, Bread Van set up his own business. A pretty damned successful one too, as I said. A bakery. Yes, I know.

A year or two of living with Angie, though, and he had eventually lost a shed load of weight and become quite the Dapper Dan. A man about town. A man of power and influence with a penchant for designer clothes. And he looked as miserable as sin.

"Give me a few minutes, Ordy," said Bardsley.

I nodded and ordered two pints of Stella and a pint of Strongbow. When I took them over to a table in the corner, Bryn and Craig were deep in conversation. Well, bickering, as usual.

"You remember Bob Grant, don't you, Ordy?" said Bryn.

"Do I?" I said.

"Of course you do. The actor. He played Jacko, the bus conductor, in that sitcom *On The Buses*. The one with fat Olive who was supposed to be as fit as a butcher's dog in real life?"

"I do indeed," I said. I gulped my pint and spilled some down my shirt.

Bryn looked at me with distaste.

"Sloppy bugger," he said.

"Ha! Hello Mr Pot, I'd like to introduce you to Mr Kettle!"

"Yeah, anyway. Back to Bob Grant. He was well

famous once upon a time. Not as famous as Reg Varney..."

"Who was the first man in Britain to use a cash machine," interrupted Craig.

Bryn shook his head.

"Well, one year, long after the show had been cancelled, he was doing a shit panto in some town out in the sticks. He only managed two shows, though, and then he did a runner. Went missing. Completely AWOL. He was eventually tracked down by a couple of News Of The Screws reporters in a run-down guest house somewhere on the south coast. Apparently, he was stressed out and depressed about being typecast as Jacko." Bryn started chewing on a roll up. "And do you know what he told the reporter?"

"Haven't a clue," I said.

"What he said was this: I felt like throwing myself under a bus. Ironic, isn't it?"

Bryn started to guffaw, spraying the table with Stella and Bombay Mix.

"Funny, or what?" he said.

"Aye. Maybe," said Craig. "But..."

Bryn and I cringed. Craig was a mine of useless information and an autodidact who was as addicted to learning a new word a day as he was to booze and drugs. I think my mum's Readers Digests did him more damage than his first pint.

"Is it a big but, Craig?" said Bryn.

Craig ignored him.

"Listen. That particular incident, and Bread Van becoming a baker after getting knocked over by a baker's van, isn't actually ironic, actually. That's not irony.

That's not what irony is. It's a very misunderstood and misused word," Craig said.

"Is that a fact?" said Bryn. He exaggerated a yawn.

"It is," said Craig.

"What is it then?" said Bryn, fidgeting. Eager to rush outside the pub for a gasper. "What is irony?"

"Well, irony's a device from the old Greek theatre. It's when the audience knows more about what's happening than a character and knows that the character's making a mistake. That's irony."

"Well, there's no need to be so *pendantic*," said Bryn. He finished his drink.

"It's pedantic actually," said Craig.

"Arf. I'll get them in before I go outside for a breath of fresh air,' said Bryn.

'What's your poisons? Same again?"

"Yep," I said. Craig gave a thumbs up and finished off his pint.

We both watched as a young woman walked over to the Wurlitzer jukebox.

She was tall with long dyed red hair, a ripped black t-shirt, high heels, leather skirt and fishnet stockings. Craig's jaw dropped so much that you could have scraped carpet fluff from his bottom lip.

The brunette started to dance to David Bowie's *Fame*. Craig couldn't take his eyes off her. Greg Bardsley wandered over and sat next to us.

"Don't even think it," said Bardsley. "That's Lightning Jones. She's way out of your league, gents. She wouldn't touch either of you with Roman Polanski or any other five foot Pole."

Craig glared at him, his eyes turning black.

I shrugged, thinking about the rent I owed. Needs must.

"So what's the story, Jackanory?" I said.

"I want you to find my dad," he said.

"Your dad?"

I was a bit taken aback since, as far as I knew, Billy Bardsley was running a protection racket somewhere near Durham. And, as such, he was persona non grata in the Bardsley home.

"Listen," said Bardsley, leaning forward and dumping his sleeve in an ashtray. "Did I ever tell you how my old man ended up doing a bunk?"

The final time Billy Bardsley had hit his wife, he'd picked up a kitchen bench and slammed it against the back of her head. Dusty had immediately reacted by slashing at Billy with a serrated knife she'd been using to gut the fish that he'd brought back from the docks. She must have hit an artery, it seems, because blood spurted out like a geyser. So much so, that Billy panicked and ran a quarter of a mile to the General Hospital, they said, just in time.

Feeling guilty, Dusty went up to the hospital the next day but he'd already checked himself out and she never saw him again. Dusty had brought young Greg up well enough on her own and he'd never been particularly curious about Billy but recently, with his wedding to Angie looming, he'd started to wonder where his old dad was and what he was up to. He even thought that maybe he should try to rekindle the father/son relationship.

When Greg had suggested this to Dusty, however, she hadn't exactly taken to the idea.

"She went mental," said Greg. "Doolally. Nearly lost the plot. And then she told me summit weird."

***

A common misconception about Private Investigators was that they we all had oodles of connections in the police force and the underworld that we used to help with our cases: for example, to track down a missing person. Well, maybe that was true of some PIs, but in my cases I had to use other resources. Like Mrs Kapuszinska.

With my eyes closed, the incense smelled even stronger and was making me feel a tad queasy. Having Big Mark Nowak's massive, clammy hand clasped in mine wasn't exactly helping things either.

This wasn't my first séance but I hoped it would be my last. Mrs Kapuszinska had told Big Mark that she'd help me if we helped her, by taking part in the séance, so here we were. And, for the most part, it was how I'd imagined a séance to be.

It was a dark cramped room with an old grandfather clock and stuffed animals. All four of us were in a circle holding hands. The four us being me, Mark Nowak, Mrs Kapuszinska – resplendent in colourful, silk robes and a turban – and the showbiz has – been, Jimmy Golden. Mrs Kapuszinska had started the proceedings by lighting incense and chanting something unintelligible, which was also as expected. The only thing that seemed out of place to me was the music.

I'd always considered myself to have a pretty strong imagination, but in my wildest dreams I'd never have thought that the best sounds to use to contact the dead would be a techno version of *Eye Of The Tiger*. Really, you learn something new every day.

The whole experience had lasted around fifteen minutes and it seemed that, through Mrs Kapuszinska, Jimmy had received another message from his late mother, who had once again told him to give up his dream of going to Las Vegas and stay put in Seatown, and go back to hairdressing. This resulted in Jimmy crying like a baby, so I assumed that it wasn't the answer he was looking for.

When the lights came on, Mrs Kapuszinska ushered

Jimmy out of the door, after taking a decent-sized wad of dosh from him. She escorted us over to a mini-bar in the corner of the room, below a stuffed owl.

"Here you are," said Mrs Kapuszinska, in an accent so sharp it could have been used in a slaughterhouse. She poured three shots of vodka.

"Na zdrowia!" said Mark, and we knocked them down in one.

For the next few minutes, Mark and Mrs Kapuszinska chattered away in Polish. Mark was massive, but very deferential to the diminutive Mrs Kapuszinska. I let them get on with it. Mrs Kapuszinska was as good a source of information as you could get. If anyone could help me track down Greg Bardsley's dad, then she could. The séance business gave her access to all sorts of information.

I checked the messages on my mobile. There was a text from Greg asking me to call him and another Jimmy Savile joke from Bryn, which I really didn't understand. I was lost in thought trying to work out the joke, and I came to when I heard Mark and Mrs Kapuszinska laughing. By the looks of things, they were discussing the design of my business card. A very subjective thing, art.

Mr Kapuszinska poured another round of drinks.

"Cheers," she said. We knocked back the vodka and it burned.

"Bimber," said Mrs Kapuszinska.

"What's that?" I said.

"Bimber," said Mark. "Polish moonshine."

"One for the road?" said Mrs Kapuszinska.

"Oh, yes," I said. And what a long and winding road that was, I can tell you.

***

Apparently, the writer Raymond Chandler once said that a piece of writing should always lead the writer and not be led by the writer. Well, it certainly worked best that way when it came to boozing. When you let the alcohol lead you, when it took the reins and dragged you with it toward the abyss, those were the best drinking sessions.

After I found out where Ernie Teal lived, I let the gargle lead me all the way to yet another stinking hangover.

Next day, I was as rough as toast, and was probably still over the limit, when I drove Trigger, my lime green Vespa, up the hill toward the Happy Valley Caravan Site.

I hadn't been there for a while but I used to be a bit of a regular at the Happy Valley Social Club back in the eighties. And, with enough booze inside me, I could regularly be convinced to belt out a version of *What's New Pussycat?* Or ten.

Those were the days before karaoke, of course. Back then, the musical entertainment in most pubs and clubs was Bandbox and consisted of a singer and an organist. Maybe a drum machine, if they were hi-tech. The performer I remember most clearly was known as Legs, an old bloke in a World War One Kaiser Bill helmet who did 'humorous' versions of popular songs. The way he transformed *The Lady In Red* into The Lady In Bed was a stroke of comic genius.

I pulled up beside Booze N News and locked up the bike.

I went into the shop and bought a can of orange Tango. A super tall Sikh with a curly goatee stood behind the counter eating a Pot Noodle.

"Scuse me mate," I said, and opened the can, spilling a little. "Do you know where a gadgy called Ernie Teal lives?"

"Why aye," he said, in a strong Geordie accent. "Who's asking? Uncle Ernie's not fussed about visitors."

And so I told him.

"Aye, well fair do's. Ernie's caravan's the one at the end. The one with the ripped Italian flag flying above it."

"Ta much," I said.

"Hold on, though. It'll be open, so just walk in, but you'd best be taking Ernie one of these as a peace offering if you want anything from him."

He tapped a bottle of Famous Grouse Whisky.

"Fair do's," I said. "I could do with a little eye opener myself."

I walked up to the caravan and knocked.

Nothing.

I knocked again and walked in.

The caravan was old and creaky but clean, albeit a bit on the sparse side.

There was a plasma television showing a darts tournament that was apparently beamed live from a seven star hotel in Dubai. A small fridge, that looked like the ones you found in hotel rooms, had a small transistor radio plonked on the top. A round coffee table and a couple of kitchen chairs were next to the window. And there was a bed. Which was where Ernie Teal lay, smothered in thick blankets that were pulled up to his chin.

Unshaven, older than the photo that I'd seen but still with a thick head of curly black hair.

I introduced myself, poured Ernie a plastic beaker of Famous Grouse and slowly sipped at mine. I was trying to control my breathing. The caravan had a smell which was similar to the one that came from the Chunky Chicken Factory when the pipes burst, and it wasn't helping my hangover a great deal.

A local station leaked out of the radio and Elton

John sang about the blues, something Ernie seemed to know a lot about, it turned out. He was guarded at first but after a couple of drinks the words tumbled out of Ernie's mouth like a gang of drunks staggering out of a pub at closing time: disorderly and unruly. And more than a little scary.

"I tell you, son. Never get old. You don't know what it's like. You know, when I close my eyes," Ernie said, shifting his stained pillow. "I can see the rain seeping into the roof... I see that dark patch spreading, you know?" he pointed a wobbly finger upwards.

I nodded.

"Sometimes I think, I can see the ceiling buckling. And when I fall asleep, I dream of drowning. Or I dream of the ceiling collapsing and filling the room with filthy water. Choking me. Dragging me under. You know what I mean?"

"Oh, aye," I said.

And he went on. And on. And on.

He said that he sometimes worried that the candles that he used to light the caravan would burn the place down. Which wouldn't have been that bad an idea if the place had still been insured. But he'd stopped the insurance payments over a year before. His pension didn't go far, after all. He had his essentials, though.

"Booze, of course, and Pot Noodles. Maybe the odd cheese and onion pie."

When the winter kicked in, his arthritis bit like a beast and he stayed in bed as much as possible, with a bottle of whisky as a teddy bear.

The whisky was his friend most of the time. Bringing him welcome memories. The golden days.

"Ernie Teal, Tommy Morten and Harjit Singh. The Rat Pack mark two. Our tribute act was the best in Seatown," he said. "Maybe the whole of the north east coast of England. We once opened for Tommy Cooper. And Shirley Bassey was a big fan, too. We played the best hotels and top night clubs. Casinos, even. Tommy was Frank. Harjit was

Sammy and I was Dean, of course. We were like kings in those days. Things were going great until that tour of the Greek Islands. You know?"

I nodded.

"Bit of a let-down, was it?" I said.

Ernie scowled and supped more whisky.

"It was a joy to start off with," he said. "The audience lapped it up night after night."

"And then some little twat of a waiter sneaked into the dressing room and took a picture of Lou Lou – the Philippine girl that did Judy Garland in the show – down on her knees, between my legs, playing Come Blow Your Horn. It was all over the tabloids in a week. Turned out that Lou Lou was only 17. And she was actually a he. How the bollocks was I to know? Eh?"

He coughed and knocked back more whisky.

"I was a laughing stock. When we played gigs the audience started shouting out requests for Lola or Dude Looks Like A Lady. So the lads sacked me. Gave me the friggin' elbow. I was devastated. Of course, I'd never been one to save money. I lived for the moment, just like Dino. But then my health took a turn for the worse.

The doctors were bloody useless. Told me to stop drinking. Said, if I didn't, I'd lose a leg to gangrene. Or maybe both. I didn't care. I kept on boozing.

And when the time came, I let them do it, without a word of protest. Let them lob my pins off. I wasn't going anywhere, was I?"

I topped up my tumbler and let Ernie go on. And he did. He really did.

"The Social Services used to send a nurse once a week. Meals on wheels, too," he said, coughing again as the whisky went down the wrong way. "But that's stopped. This is the Big Society, they said. My friends and family would have to help me. No wonder they called it BS," he said.

"What about the rest of the act?"

"Tommy and Harjit are in London now, working with that Jonathon Ross on his television show. It's ironic humour, apparently. The pay's serious enough, though.

I could have been there. If I could walk."

He guzzled the last of the whisky from the tumbler. I topped him up. The bottle was emptying PDQ. Ernie must have read my mind.

"Don't worry, lad. Mrs Griffiths from the corner shop will be here in a while with the new supply. She's a bit on the big side but she's alright. She laughs when I sing That's Amore but not so much when my teeth fall out. And then, if my lucks in, she crawls into bed with me"

He winked.

I smiled, approvingly.

"Like Dino said: everybody loves somebody, sometime," he said.

And if I wasn't feeling depressed enough then, the look on his face when I told him about Greg Bardsley poured another cup's worth into the pool of misery. It was going to be a long day.

The evening was melting into a tar-coloured night as I walked home. The aftermath of meeting Ernie Teal had left me draped in gloom and contemplating forming a tribute band of my own. Maybe Joy Division. Or Nirvana.

***

A bitter January had bled into a rain-drenched February and private detective jobs were few and far between. Until Jack Martin called.

When I walked into Jack's office at Velvettes, I was expecting a bollocking after my shenanigans with Maria the stripper, and wasn't exactly expecting to be hired to find the Rara Avis. Still...

"A babysitter?" I said.

Jack glared at me, his blue eyes piercing beetroot skin.

"You used to be a schoolmaster, right?" he said, filling two tumblers with brandy. "Before you got into the gumshoe game?"

"Once upon a time," I said. "When dinosaurs walked the earth."

I thought back to the staff room at Dyke House Comprehensive School, stuffed to the brim with disappointment, underachievement and cigarette smoke, and was immediately draped in a cloak of gloom. I gulped my brandy.

"English I believe?" said Jack, lighting a King Edward cigar.

I nodded.

"Right, well. Listen. My daughter, my little angel, Holly, is doing her A Levels at the moment and isn't doing so well at the subject. She can't tell King Lear from a pig's ear. The lives of dead poets hold bugger all interest for her. So I've decided that you can give her a little extra tutorial, while I'm away on my hols in Lansagrotty."

"But why me? There must be lots of eager…"

Jack held up a hand.

"Yes, well, maybe too eager, some of them," he said. "My Holly's a beautiful young girl and I don't want anyone trying to have their wicked way with her while I'm away. She needs to concentrate on her studies. Her future. So, yes, as well as helping with her stanzas and whatnot you can keep an eye out for any unsavoury characters.

You'll be like a night watchman."

I shuffled in my seat.

"So, the English lessons are just a cover?" I said.

"Not much gets past you, lad," said Jack.

He chuckled to himself, picked up a copy of the Times and started on the crossword. Nothing like an ego boost to start the day.

Later that night, I was nestled on a bar stool contemplating the evening's third double whisky. Uncharacteristically, The Raby Arms was heaving and, unfortunately, so was the man next to me.

"Paddy, watch what you're doing," I said, stepping away from the pool of pavement pizza.

"Sorry, brother," said Paddy.

I moved closer to the bar. Tuc was in full on seventies disco mode, playing Sheila & B. Devotions' Spacer. A bunch of sweaty Muscle Marys, on their way to Newcastle to see Dame Shirley Bassey, were knocking back shots of Tequila.

"So, Tuc. What can you tell me about Jack Martin's daughter, Holly?"

"Holly? The Princess Of Seatown? Spoilt little twat, if you ask me. Even worse since poor Mrs. Martin popped her clogs, God rest her soul. She looks like butter wouldn't melt in her mouth but I've heard that a few chav stiffies certainly have. They don't call her Minstrels for nothing."

"Oh, great," I said, wringing out the sleeve of my jacket, which I'd just plonked in a pool of beer.

"Yeah," said Tuc. "And I've also heard she's got a thing for older men. So you better watch your step."

"Aye," I said. "Fingers and legs crossed. See you

later."

I stepped out into the cold night air and flagged down a taxi.

The fart smelling taxi snaked its way outside the town, behind the park, where the buses don't run, towards a six bedroom mock Tudor house. There really was a

lot of dosh in this world, but none of it was in my pocket and the resentment gurgled in my gut as the taxi stuttered to a full stop outside a swinging sign: Dun Robbin.

I paid the taxi driver, walked up to the house and rang the doorbell.

The door was opened by a petite, short-haired blonde in a Cradle Of Filth t-shirt and cut-off jeans tight enough for you to be able to read her lips.

"Holly," I said. "I'm Peter Ord."

"Follow me, Mr Teacher," she said and she led me into a house so kitsch that Liberace would consider it tasteless.

"Help yourself to a drink," said Holly. "And I'll slip into something more comfortable."

As she bounded upstairs, I did just that. Jack Martin's white globe drinks cabinet might have been tacky but it was well stocked. I poured myself a large vodka and had a sniff around for some fruit juice.

After a couple of minutes, dressed exactly the same, Holly bounded back down the stairs with a pile of books and sat next to me on the sofa.

"This is cosy, isn't it?" she said. I swigged the vodka to wash away the dark and dingy thoughts that were lurking in the murky corners of my mind and immediately an old Police song corkscrewed through my brain. And it wasn't the one about a message in a bottle.

***

One week later, Jack Martin was back from his holidays and I headed down to Velvettes for my pay.

"You did surprisingly well, lad," said Jack, his skin looking weirdly bronzed. Reminded me of barbecued sausage. "After the... *faux pas*... you had with that lap dancer, I wasn't 100% sure that you could be trusted, but... well, the CCTV speaks for itself."

Jack started counting out the wad of cash.

"I could see it all. The only visitor my angel had was that Carole Parker girl from school. And they just stayed in her room studying until the early hours, not even a trip to a nightclub."

As I put the money into my jacket pocket, I had a flashback to the night I'd drunk too much and fallen asleep on the sofa at Jack's house. This segued into me going looking for the toilet, accidentally walking into Holly's bedroom and finding her and Carole involved in what the tabloids would call Girl-On-Girl Love Action.

"Let's hope she passes her exams," I said, finishing off my brandy.

Jack grinned.

"No need to worry about that," he said. 'The head of the local education department is a regular in Velvettes. He owes me big time after a recent... indiscretion.'

"Well, it's not what you know, it's who you know," I said, and scarpered as quickly as possible.

***

The trouble with me was that I never realised how deep in the shit I was until I was choking on the stuff and I'd thought that getting back in Jack Martin's good books was a good thing. I really did. Well, you know what thought did, as my old gran used to say.

Still, he spread the word around and I picked up a bit more work here and there. Some good payers too.

It was coming up to Valentine's Day, traditionally one of the Samaritans' busiest nights. The moon grasped the dawn sky and seagulls screeched and cackled through the roaring wind as a long-limbed blonde tripped out of the large Georgian house in Burlington Park Road and into an idling yellow taxi. Shivering, I shuffled onto Trigger and followed – making shortcuts down alleyways and across supermarket car parks – before catching up to the cab as it pulled up outside 66 Jackson's Wharf, one of the Marina's many luxury apartments.

I pulled off my piss-pot cyclist's helmet and scratched my itchy head. I clapped my hands and stamped my feet to keep warm. After about twenty minutes, Beavis & Butthead began the elongated chuckle that signalled that I had a text message.

It was from Bobby.

SHE'S IN BED. COME UP.

Bobby Bowles was a former Newcastle United striker who had royally screwed up his glittering future when he'd knocked over a seventy-year-old woman while driving home from a nightclub, pissed as a fart. He was tabloid fodder for months.

As it turned out, the old woman only suffered a few cuts and bruises while Bobby ended up with a head injury, a stroke and a career flushed down the Swanee River.

He buzzed me into the flat and I took the lift to the top floor. Bobby sat in an electric wheelchair wearing silk pyjamas and sipping whisky. He was only forty but he looked much older, with a brow so furrowed it looked as if his forehead had collapsed.

"Help yourself to a gargle," he croaked.

I poured myself a large Jim Beam, and looked around the room enviously.

The rumours were that Bowles' walking problem was psychosomatic, all in his head. Induced by guilt. Whatever the cause, he was almost a recluse these days, like a downmarket Howard Hughes.

I sat on the massive black leather sofa and sipped my drink. Bowles put an envelope containing my fee on the table in front of him and glared at me.

"Well?" he said.

Bowles had hired me because he was convinced that Louise, his wife – who the red tops, in a rare moment of veracity, had described as 'young and vivacious' – was playing away from home. After a couple of weeks of being a Peeping Tom, however, it became apparent to me that Bowles had put two and two together and made sixty-nine.

However, when I told him what she was really doing... well, he turned albino white.

"A care assistant?" he said. His hand shook as he gulped his whisky.

"Yep," I said.

"Looking after old dears? Wiping their arses, and that?"

I nodded, stifling a yawn.

I'd got Mrs Bowles sister drunk at the weekend, and she'd told me that that the insurance he was receiving after his car accident didn't cover his luxury lifestyle so his wife had got a part time job to make ends meet. She'd kept it a secret from Bobby because she didn't want him to feel useless and impotent. Ain't love grand?

Bowles shook his head and started to sob.

"My Sugarcube," he moaned, and put his head in his hands.

I finished my drink, picked up my payment, and left. I had another meeting with Jack the next day.

***

Jack Martin had started attending an anger management course shortly after his first heart attack and he felt he'd achieved a modicum of success in a fairly short time, although Ricky Starr would probably have begged to differ. Or rather, I'm sure he would have at least begged, if he hadn't been hindered by the jumbo pork pie that was stuffed in his mouth and the fishing wire that bound his wrists and ankles.

"You like porkies, I'll give you porkies," yelled Jack, red-faced and spitting.

I sat in a black leather armchair – just like the one on Mastermind – gazing nervously out of the window of Starr's spacious loft apartment. A storm beat the morning sky black and blue, and I wondered what it was with minor celebrities and black leather furniture.

Starr was a real suntanned medallion man. He'd written a few Eurovision

Song Contest contenders back in the 70s and managed Black Lace – just before the singer was arrested for knobbing an under-age girl. He'd made a few bob, too, which he invested in slot machine 'salons'. At some point or other he'd been drawn into Jack Martin's orbit, like so many people in the town.

"You are a lying toe rag and a lying, thieving toe rag to boot," said Jack, slamming down his whisky tumbler so hard the ice cubes almost jumped out of the glass.

"Where are my ladies?" he said, trying to control his

breathing and squeezing a rubber tennis ball.

"You better tell me or you'll be doing a Steve Bilko out of that window."

I stood up and walked out on to the balcony to get some air. I'd worked for

Jack a few more times over the last few weeks but I'd never been this close to his nefarious activities.

Starr's eyes bulged. He nodded his head furiously.

"Well?" said Jack.

"Gag gugga," said Starr

"What?" said Jack.

"Gag gugga," said the red faced Starr, looking like he was about to burst.

Jack held his breath and exhaled. Then he stormed forward with a knife in his hand. Starr struggle and tried to scream but Jack thrust the knife forward into the pork pie. He pulled it out, the pie almost in one piece, spilling only a few chunks down Ricky Starr's sweat-stained Armani shirt. Starr wheezed and farted.

"Again," said Jack.

Tears in his eyes, Starr gasped for breath.

"The Headland," he rasped.

***

Angie's smile was like the froth on a cappuccino. It softened and took the edge off the darkness and bitterness beneath it. Well, if you didn't know her.

My ex-wife was standing at the foot of my bed in shiny, black riding boots and a tight, tweed jacket that accentuated her cleavage. Her blonde hair caught the traces of sunlight that peeked through the lace net curtains. Specks of dust floated in a shard of sunlight. She held a large brown envelope in her right hand, which she held just six inches in front of my sweaty, stubbly chin.

And yes, my little soldier was standing to attention alright, but that was because I'd just woken up; not because of Angie. Not this time. Honest.

"A pleasant sight for an early riser," I croaked, as I shuffled up onto my elbows, my stiffy thankfully dwindling.

Angie said nothing, though. She just stood there, her grin frozen, like her plastic surgery had gone horribly wrong.

"From Greg," she said. "Though why he employed a useless pillock like you, I can't think."

"Can you put it on the rocking chair?" I said.

Angie grunted and walked over to the debris-littered rocking chair in the corner of the room. The tidiest spot, however.

She dropped the envelope overly loudly, spilling whatever else had been dumped there. Coins clattered onto the wooden floorboards. Cacophonous was the word that came to mind.

As she looked contemptuously around the room, her eyes stopped at the dust-coated door that was propped up against the wall. Peter Ord – Private Investigator was written on the frosted glass. I'd bought it when I'd decided to become a Private Eye.

I was just waiting for the office.

"Ever the overachiever, eh Peter?" she said. And walked out, slamming the bedroom door behind her.

My already frail ego had another kicking. It was a time for action, I knew. I had to take control of my life. To be proactive. Self-motivated.

So, I sipped the dregs from one of the cans of lager, thought about Angie, and knocked one out before drifting into a dead sleep.

***

The night was as cold as a shop-soiled spinster. I paid the taxi driver, got a receipt and gave him a tip, which didn't seem to impress him. I headed into the Headland Hotel, which looked like a converted palace and was situated in a renovated and gentrified area that used to be Seatown docks.

A tall, blonde receptionist with a 1000-watt smile grinned as I went to the bar to meet Jack Martin's contact.

The KuntaKinte blonde sitting at the corner of the bar was looking a little tipsy, though she was more than a tad tasty despite that. She was wearing a red leather dress that was made with just about enough material to make a wallet, and looking like a long limbed drink of water calling out to a thirsty man. And I was parched.

"Moira?" I said, holding out my hand.

"And you would be...?" she purred, scrutinising me, as if she were looking at a magic eye painting.

"Peter Ord," I said. I gave her a card.

She raised her eyebrows, clearly unimpressed.

"What can I get you to drink?" I said.

"Is Jack paying for this?"

"Yep," I said. He hadn't trusted me enough to give me cash but the expenses limit was pretty high.

"G and T," she said.

"Ice and a slice?"

"Aye."

"I'll have the same," I said to the metrosexual barman, who looked like he was nodding off.

"We've got no ice," he said, scratching his head and powdering his black, velvet waistcoat with dandruff.

"If you want to chill your drink you can hold it against my ex-wife's heart," I said.

Moira cracked a smile.

"How long were you hitched?" she said.

"I dunno," I said. "How long does chloroform take to wear off?"

She laughed loudly and we made a toast to freedom. The night melted into morning and the conversation flowed just as much as the booze.

I woke up to the sound of seagulls screeching. Memories fizzed like champagne bubbles. I looked at the clock radio next to the bed. It was almost mid-day and Moira had already left. I dressed quickly and unsteadily headed downstairs. She was waiting in the car park.

As soon as I saw her my heart did a Keith Moon drum solo.

"Your chariot awaits," she said, banging on the roof of a dirty white transit van with the sign 'Kowalski Plumbers, 23hr Service' on the side. Someone had drawn a pair of tits in the dust.

"Wanna gander at the merchandise," said Moira.

"Why not," I said. She opened up the back doors and jemmied open a wooden box to reveal a pile of small statuettes of the Virgin Mary.

"Packed with the white powder, they are. Jack got them from Columbia and sent them to Poland thinking that, in such big Catholic countries, no one would interfere with Holy Mary, eh? But they were hijacked near Gdansk and ended up here."

My stomach rumbled like a German tank rolling into Warsaw.

"I'm hungry," I said. "Is there anywhere around here where I can get a takeaway?"

"Not a lot around here," said Moira. "Except posh restaurants. Maybe something on your way to Jack's."

I leaned forward to give her a kiss but she waved

me away.

"Happy trails," she said, and she was into her Mercedes and off into the distance like the Lone Ranger. I'd spotted a Chinese fish and chip shop on my way out of the city and managed to get a bag of chips and couple of battered Mars bars which I wolfed down.

A few minutes later, I was feeling decidedly queasy so I decided to stop off at my flat for a tactical puke before going to see Jack. I pulled up close to the art deco clock tower and was locking up the van when I heard a ragged voice.

"Ord?"

I turned and saw a Frank Stallone lookalike in an expensive-looking raincoat stumble toward me.

"Yeah," I said. "Who's asking?"

He rushed closer and threw a punch that hit the side of my head.

"Shit!" I said.

I pushed him backwards into the window of Berny The Bolt's DVD Rentals Shop, which cracked as he crashed into it.

"You twat," he said, as he charged towards me, red faced.

He barged me towards an alley at the back of the off license. Gasping for breath, I hurtled into a pile of stuffed and overflowing black bin bags that spilled across the alley. I felt as if I'd been in this situation before.

A drunken Cupid, complete with wings and a bow and arrow, was trying to piss against a wheely-bin. He was singing:

"Oh, Ruby! Don't take your knickers down."

I started to puke.

"You dirty bastard," said Cupid, zipping up his fly and collecting his kebab from the top of a wheelie bin.

Stallone staggered into him.

"Yer fucker," said Cupid, wobbling like a stoned Weeble and pushing Stallone away.

Frank Stallone rushed towards me and then he slipped on my pool of vomit, fell forward and banged his head. Out cold.

"Fucker," said Cupid who rushed forward and started kicking Stallone in the balls.

"Yer gunner call the filth?" said Cupid. "He's a wrong 'un he is."

Shit, I thought, best not. Not with all that happy talc in the van. I pulled out my phone and called Jack Martin.

"Ey, hang on, I know him," said Cupid shuffling up to me, moving in close and conspiratorially like a double-agent in a Harry Palmer film. I held my breath.

"He used to be the Sunderland captain. When they weren't shit, like."

"Narrows it down," I said. "Narrows it down."

***

The recession clearly hadn't hit Astros Bar, which was surprisingly packed for a Tuesday lunchtime. Tuc and I were lucky to find a table near the stinky toilets.

"Here," said Tuc. "From Jack."

He handed me a large brown envelope.

"Jack said that you did a good job bringing back his 'ladies' but he's made deductions for clearing up the mess with your footballer friend this afternoon," he said.

"What was the score with him, anyway?" Tuc said, grinning.

"Yes, score, footballer, very good" I said.

I sipped my drink.

"Well," I said. "It turned out that Bowles' wife actually was shagging someone else."

"With a footballer? Playing away from home?"

"Ahem. Yes. The owner of the old people's homes was Tony 'Mad Dog' Sheldon, ex-1972 Sunderland FA Cup squad."

I wiped the froth from my top lip.

"Bowles found out," I continued, 'and gave his wife an ultimatum. Him or me. She packed her bags and went to Sheldon who was none too pleased about his bit on the side turning up on his doorstep. Neither was his wife. So, the shit hit the fan and heated arguments and heavy drinking ensued. The upshot of which was that Tony Sheldon decided to take it out on me.'

Patsy, the barmaid, brought a plate of vegetable curry and rice over and placed it in front of Tuc.

"Thanks, Patsy," he said.

"Pub grub?" I said, aghast. "In Astros?!"

"Yep, Kenny and Browny are turning Astros into a Gastropub, ain't they?"

"Pub meals!" I said, looking around Astros. "A 20th century abomination. It used to be that you could pop into the pub at lunch time for a swift half or an emergency pint and the place was half empty. Now, look. You can't get served because the place is full of pasty faced, salad munching secretaries ordering coffee," I said.

"Don't moan at me," said Tuc. "Speak to him."

I gazed across the room. Kenny Cokehead, AKA Kenny Ratface, and John The Con were engaged in a heated discussion at the corner of the bar.

"They're not your proper friends, John. They're not your mates, mate," said Kenny Cokehead.

He paced up and down in front of the bar, waving his arms around like a demented ninja throwing shuriken.

"Them lot on that Facefuck and Twatter an' that. On that computer an' that."

He jabbed a finger at John The Con's iPad.

"They're not your proper mates. We're your proper mates. Me and Browny and…" Kenny stretched out a wobbly arm and gestured around Astros Bar "…this lot. They're your muckers. Him with the syrup, Lip Up Fatty, Scotch Barry and him with the lisp that's good at the quiz machines. We're your proper mates."

John the Con just ignored Kenny and continued to update his Facebook status.

And it seemed that this was what was annoying Kenny. The fact that John The Con, who used to be in Astros Bar eight days out of seven, now spent most of his weekends at home, 'networking'. John had been a fair-to-middling fence, back in the day.

But the introduction of social networking had helped him to start shifting a load of high-class stuff and improve his market share. Apparently.

"I mean, us lot, we're like family. Remember that night when Hedgehog Eddie choked on a pickled onion? We were all there that night. Eh? And next day we had to get round to his flat and clean out his porn stash before his mam saw it? That's mates! Eh? Eh?"

John took a gulp of *7-Up*, crunched the ice cubes between his teeth.

"Eh? I'm right, aren't I? Eh?' I am, eh, Ordy?"

He stuck his sweaty face in front of mine.

I opened a bag of pork scratchings.

"You've certainly got a point, I'll give you that," I said.

"See, John? See? I'm right," said Kenny, spraying spittle "You can't argue you with me, can you? Got no answer for it. Nowt to say, eh? Answer that?"

John put his iPad into his man bag. Stroked his Zapata moustache.

"A wise man speaks because he has something to say," said John. "A stupid man speaks because he has to say something."

Kenny looked at John. Squinted and turned to me.

"Is he calling me a cunt?"

***

The Blue Anchor on a drizzly afternoon was usually about as lively as a Coldplay song and today was no exception. I was zoning out from the barflies' heated conversations – the smoking ban, for about the thousandth time – and staring at the big silver star that hung above the bar all year round; day in, day out. It dangled slightly askew, just to the left of the Seatown United clock. Its tinsel border had pretty much moulted to almost nothing and the glittery red Merry Xmas greeting had dandruffed so many barflies over the years that it was almost unreadable.

But I remembered the night that Mad Frank had hung it up. Or, to be more precise, got someone else to hang it up. Frank was a corpulent slug who rarely moved from his fart-draped stool at the end of the bar and spent most of his nights glaring at staff and customers alike. This was a man who once barred someone out of the pub for laughing too loud and was universally loathed – a fact that seemed to give him pleasure; if, indeed, Frank was capable of pleasure.

Frank was also as tight as a gnat's arse and, only hours after he was found dead behind the bar, some wag had quipped that he'd died of a heart attack after finding a foreign coin in the till. But I knew why Tommy, Frank's brother, kept the star hanging there, long after he'd taken over as the pub's landlord.

It was a reminder. A reminder of the fact that no matter what he'd done, or would do, he would never be as big a twat as Frank.

"Merry Xmas, brother," said Tommy each Xmas Day with the flicker of a grin on his ruddy face as he remembered the fateful and fatal Christmas cracker that put Frank out of his own and everyone else's misery.

Tommy sat next to me looking like he was carrying a heavy weight, and that wasn't just the massive fry up he'd brought from the kitchen.

"No one gets out of life without dirtying their hands, Tommy," I said, watching the steam rise from his muddy coffee. Tommy just nodded and started digging into his bacon and eggs with all the enthusiasm of an ex-con in a bordello.

The pub was stiflingly hot. Behind the bar, Madge, a midget with a withered arm, who had just moved back home after a stint running a dwarves escort agency in London, was serving dark brown beer with a frothy head to a couple of Teddy Boys with fading tattoos. A sound system that was twice as big as Madge blasted out a Gary Newman song.

"I've gone arse over tit many a time, metaphorically and literally," I said.

"Especially when I've been imbibing."

Tommy picked up a napkin and shined his pearl Yin and Yang cuff links.

Sitting back in his chair, he flicked lint from his black Hugo Boss suit, surveyed the room disinterestedly and then gave me a look of consternation. He looked into his lap.

Tommy was an overweight man in his late sixties with an expression so hangdog as to make a basset hound jealous. He absently scratched his arm with a fork.

Without looking up, he said:

"So, do you believe me?"

"I'm a... facilitator," I said, squirming as Tommy pulled a string of bacon rind from his mouth. "I'm impartial. It matters not a jot if I believe you or not. My responsibility is to listen to your story. And to act."

Tommy stared out of the window at Seatown High Street, which was bustling with shoppers. A group of school kids raced past, chased by a wheezing Cupid.

"So. Tommy. Take it away. From the top. One more time," I said.

"Well, you see, I put it down to stress," said Tommy, shuffling in his seat.

"Things went pear-shaped about a year ago. This recession. Worldwide crisis. You know?"

I nodded.

"I lost control of the pub. The brewery took it away from me."

"Why?"

"Well, I've always had a bit of a weight problem and I'd tried my best to keep it under control but you know... well, the brewery said I was bad for their new image. I'd been in the pub game all my life."

He let out a wheezy sigh.

"And then I kept getting this urge. This compulsion. It came during the night. In the street. I'd never felt that way before. I'd always been a clean-living kinda guy."

He downed his coffee in one.

"I was down London, in Harrods, when the urge reached a... a crescendo. I was in the food hall. And I saw them. A massive bunch of Cumberland sausages. Juicy. Succulent. I just had to have them. Before I knew it, I'd whipped them off the shelf and stuffed them down the front of my trousers."

"Ahem," I said.

"And then I just wandered off, in some sort of a trance."

"And you ended up where?"

"In the lingerie section," said Tommy.

"Aha," I said.

"I don't remember getting there. Like I say, I was in a... sort of a ..."

"Trance. Yes, you did say."

"I came to when this vinegary-looking woman started screaming at me.

Calling me a pervert."

"What happened?"

"I looked down and realized that my fly was half open and one of the sausages was sticking out. The security guards came and then the police and then I was charged. With... with ..."

"With indecent exposure?"

Tommy nodded. Madge plonked a plate of apple pie and custard in front of him. He started to breathe heavily.

"But I'm not a perv. If this gets out, well... You believe me, don't you? I need you to believe me, Peter."

"Strangely enough, I do," I said. "But the most important question, of course, is what I need to do to eradicate your problem and, more importantly for me, if you can afford to pay."

"I can, I can," he said. "Are you sure you can help?"

I nodded, knowing nothing of the sort. "Give me the information, the description of the woman and I'm sure I'll be able to... renegotiate with her to drop the charges."

Trembling, Tommy pushed a stuffed brown

envelope over to me.

"It's all there," he said. "Can you honestly do what you say?"

"Of course I can," I said. "I'm as honest as the day is long."

If you live in Iceland.

Tommy nodded and headed off out into the breaking storm.

I bought another pint and sat reading the Seatown Gazette, which had the usual stories about smack-heads running riot and a free supplement about even more new expensive flats that were going to be built on the Marina. The front page story, though, was about a local boy made good. One of my old schoolmates, in fact: Simon Lecher. He'd hit the big time and made a fortune by writing crime thrillers and selling them as eBooks – whatever they were – over the internet. Meanwhile, the centre pages proclaimed that Seatown's premier indie band Monkeyheaven had scored a massive international hit with the song Someone Else's Wife after it was used in the last Coen brothers' film. I was so envious that I was in danger of turning into The Incredible Hulk.

I looked up when someone sat next to me.

It was Angie and she was as pissed as a fart.

"You're as pissed as a fart," I said.

"Still attending that charm school, then?" she said.

She plonked a bottle of white wine on the table and glared at me.

"You… you," she said. "You've got the magic touch, haven't you?"

It was a familiar look so I knew I'd made a bollocks of something. I had no idea what, though. So I just let her talk.

"You're like… King Midas in reverse. Everything

you touch turns to shit!"

She poured the rest of her wine into a glass the size of a goldfish bowl, which spilled over.

And then she told me. How she had mentioned to her mother about Greg Bardsley's real dad being Ernie Teal. And how her mother started crying. It turned out Ernie had been a busy man when he lived in Seatown. He was in and out the local women like a fiddler's elbow. And had got more than a few of them up the duff. So, guess who Angie's real dad was?

That banjo picker from *Deliverance* came to mind again as Angie threw most of the glass of wine over me and rushed out of the pub into the storm. I ignored the barflies' sniggers and finished off the bottle.

***

I was more than a tad tipsy, and particularly famished, as I left The Blue Anchor, so I called in for a kebab. As soon as I got out of the sweaty kebab shop, it started raining. I spotted a yellow cab and tried to get in but the driver wouldn't open up.

"Come on, mate," I said. "I'm freezing me nads off out here." But the bushy-eyebrowed driver just shook his head and wound down his window.

"Money first," he said.

Bollocks, I thought. I had the envelope that Tommy had given me but I didn't particularly want to open that up in front of the taxi driver. There were, after all, some very unscrupulous people in Seatown.

I dug into my pocket but all I pulled out was hand full of shrapnel. The driver shook his head so I pointed over to a cash machine near the kebab shop.

"Two ticks," I said.

The thing is, I didn't usually use the hole in the wall. I pretty much always got paid in cash these days. And this was one of those fancy ones with the glass screen over the keyboard. I scratched my head for a bit and just put my bank card into the slot and mumbled,

"Open sez me!"

But then I paused: What the bollocks was my pin number? I really couldn't remember the last time I'd used the machine. My kebab was getting a bit wet, so I pushed it in the corner of the cash machine to keep it dry, and tried to think of the number.

First, I typed in my date of birth. INVALID PIN it said on the screen.

Then I punched that number backward but I got the same answer.

Well, I was flummoxed. And then, I had a moment of inspiration. The number of the beast. Plus one extra. I was sure of it. Well, everyone had their Crowley phases, didn't they?

First there was nothing and I got a bit of a sweat on. Then there was a sound. A clanging or whirring. Like in an old science fiction film when the robot comes to life. I knew something was happening. And I started to grin.

Then I looked at the screen again. INVALID PIN. CARD RETAINED – and the glass wall came down. Trapping my kebab with it too.

I turned around and saw the taxi driver shake his head before he drove off. Pulling my collar up, I set off walking.

I was outside the old and abandoned Odeon cinema, wet, cold, starving, knackered and, worst of all, sobering up, when I had to stop for a gypsy's kiss. I leaned against the peeling *Cannonball Run Two* poster and pulled out my old man. Looked up at the poster and fought back a wave of bitter cold nostalgia.

I let the piss splash on my hands a while to warm myself up, and then,

From the corner of my eye, I saw a big black car pulling up. Could have been BMW but I wasn't sure. I knew little more about cars than I did about Dutch agriculture. Apart from the Bat Mobile and Kit from Knight Rider, they all looked the same to me.

After that I was a tad stressed and couldn't go, so I zipped up and walked off, looking over my shoulder.

The car started up again and drove past, stopping about fifty yards in front of me. I slowed down my walk. When I got close to the car I could hear music playing and start to relax a bit.

"Get in," shouted Jack Martin, and I did.

"Just the man I've been looking for," said Jack, turning down Mammas, *Don't Let Your Babies Grow Up To Be Cowboys*.

Jack was dressed in a ten-gallon hat and an outrageous rhinestone shirt.

Tonight was his Line Dancing Class.

"Aye?" I said.

"Oh, aye," he said, sniffing a bit and looking me up and down.

"I've got a little job for you," he said, spraying the car with peach deodorant. I could see that I wasn't meeting Jack's high standards. I'd heard he inspected the napkins on the table before he'd eat in a greasy spoon.

"Oh, aye."

Jack turned the car onto Murray Street, past all the boarded up terraced houses. Used to be a well desirable area when I was a kid, but not now.

"What does the name 'The Nuthouse' mean to you?" said Jack.

I shrugged my shoulders.

"Well, there was that hairdressers on Church Street. Changed its name to Curl Up & Dye?"

"Friggin hell, you're going back a bit, aren't you?" said Jack. He shook his head. "You're living in the past, young man. Well, here in the twenty-first century, The Nuthouse is a pub."

He lit up an Embassy Regal, although I knew he wasn't supposed to smoke.

"A family pub. Over on the Coast Road."

"Never heard of it," I said.

"Aye," groaned Jack. "And that's just the problem."

"The town's full of fun pubs and family pubs anyway. Wacky Jacky's, Tricky

Micky's. Who'd be daft enough to open another...?"

Jack glared.

"Good location, the Coast Road. Good location," I said. "Perfect."

Jack said nothing and I started getting edgy. I tried to hum along to the music but Jack glared again so I just shut up.

"No, the place is a leech," said Jack. "Draining my savings. The worst investment that I've ever made. So, I've been pondering. I need to start work on another money-spinner. So I can leave a legacy for my Holly, should I croak."

"And what can I do to help you?" I said, eventually.

The street looked deserted but, as we got closer to the public toilets, I could see a couple of cars and a truck parked on the piece of waste ground that had been given the nickname Dogging Lane. Dogging Lane had earned itself a bit of a national reputation recently via the very popular YouTube clip of a couple of well-known kids' television presenters who were filmed there making a spit roast out of a six-foot-six transvestite known locally as Ella The Fella.

Jack slowed down, stopped the car, and turned to me.

"I want to share a secret with you," he said.

The silence dragged like a BNP voter's knuckles. I'd always had a bit of an overripe imagination but it really was working overtime now.

And then Jack completely flummoxed me when he said:

"I want you to become a ghost."

***

"Diversification is the key to success, Peter," said Jack Martin. "Remember Ann The Man?"

"Aye," I said. Ann was a massive greengrocer and money launderer who came to a very violent end a bit back.

"Well, Ann used to say that "opportunities sometimes slip through your fingers like grains of sand." Like gold dust. And then the moment's lost. Forever. And other times you've got to nudge the window of opportunity open a little bit more…"

Jack Martin and Ann's words of wisdom were very probably true. I didn't know. Didn't care. I was having problems concentrating on what he was saying.

We were jogging along the beach, just after the dawn had been cracked open like a can of *Poundland* lager. Or rather, Jack was jogging; I was struggling to catch up with him. The tide was out, revealing hundreds upon hundreds of chicken heads and feet. The Chunky Chicken factory's waste disposal pipe had broken again.

"I'm in the twilight of my years, Peter, and I need to leave something behind for my daughter Holly. Something that can't be grabbed from her hands by the thieving toe-rags in the town."

The upshot was that, inspired by Simon Lecher's eBook success, Jack wanted to write a book. A disguised autobiography that would detail his rise though the gangland ranks until he became a crime lord. The profits would go to Holly after his death, giving her a nice little nest egg. And he wanted me to be the ghost writer of the book. For a well tidy fee, too.

After Jack did another circuit on the beach he headed off home.

For three weeks afterwards, we worked on the book. Night after night.

There was a sense of urgency from Jack and I could barely keep up with his enthusiasm. But the material really was all good stuff. Jack had yarns aplenty. He talked about when he was in Captain Cutlass' mob and how they headed down to London to take on The Richardson Gang and returned with their respective tails between their legs after getting lost on the Underground. He described the secret drinking club that was at the back of an antiques shop in one of the local villages. And more. He even said where the bodies were buried. Literally.

He eventually got into the habit of staying over at my dingy flat, knocking back vodka and Red Bull and popping various pills to keep himself awake while we worked on the book.

In the early hours of one morning, however, when I awoke on my sofa, a Mel Torme song was playing at a low volume and Jack was lying on the floor foaming at the mouth like a rabid dog. And then he went into convulsions.

I drained a glass of brandy, turned over and went back to sleep.

Felt rough the next day.

The funeral was a week later. I skipped the church service and went straight to the cemetery.

"Dead centre of town," said the taxi driver when I told him where I wanted to go.

He dropped me off outside the cemetery's wrought-iron gates and I walked through the rain towards the grave. It was packed. Half of the gangsters in the town were there, including the Krugers, who glared at me. Holly was shaking, looking like a kid, her arm around Tuc, who was actually crying.

Reverend Abbott, his long hair flowing in the cold north wind, began his familiar eulogy.

"There comes a time in every young man's life,' he said, his long arms stretched wide, 'when he knows that he will never be The Fonz. Shortly after that realisation it becomes clear that he won't even be Richie Cunningham. And so, then, he has to make a choice. Will he be Ralph Malph or Potsie Weber? But there are some men..."

I tuned out after that. Reverend Abbott's frankly barmy sermons were as infamous as his acid flashbacks. It was clear where he was going, though. I patted the pen drive in my pocket. My security blanket. Jack's memoirs were pretty much finished and no one knew about his writing project except me. So, a couple of tweaks here and there and I reckoned I had a best-selling crime novel on my hands. The Guns Of Seatown by Peter S. Ord had a very nice ring to it indeed.

Like Jack had said that day on the beach, sometimes a window of opportunity was opened and you had to jump right through it, head first, if need be. And at other times... well, you just had to kick the fucker in.

As soon as the funeral was over, the clouds parted and the sun came out, looking like a big gold doubloon. And then a rainbow hung over Seatown and I set off toward it. It was almost opening time.

Mr Kiss & Tell

The last time Tommy Kirby hit his wife, he'd picked up a kitchen bench and slammed it against the back of her head. Sharon had immediately reacted by slashing at Tommy with a knife she'd been using to gut the fish that he'd brought back from the docks. She must have hit an artery, it seems, because blood spurted out like a geyser. So much so, that Tommy panicked and ran a quarter of a mile they said, just in time.

ot back home two days later,
ith their five-year-old son Nick.
ng for them.

d on, Tommy Kirby, alone in
g Association flat, like so many
ned to Mecca. Come rain or come shine,
or high water, every Monday and Friday
noon Tommy was in the Mecca Bingo. And on
Wednesdays he was in The King Johns.

It was just after opening time. I was having a break from my store detective's job at *Poundland* and I was meeting a prospective client. Billy.

Patsy, the pasty faced barmaid brought over a Full English Breakfast for Billy and the vegetarian version from me. I was on a bit of a health kick. I'd even been on the wagon for two weeks.

"It's still a heart attack on a plate," said Tommy looking down at my food.

"From little acorns," I said.

"So, when did you last hear from the family?" I said, as I cut into my Tofuburger.

Tommy shrugged his shoulders and stuffed a burned black sausage into his mouth.

"Donkeys years ago," he said, his mouth full. "Sometime in the last century, to be a bit more precise."

"Are they still in the town?"

"Apparently they are, though I heard she'd buggered off to her cousin's in Hull for a while."

"Hull hath no fury like a woman scorned," I said, smirking a little.

Tommy didn't laugh, though.

***

My beard was itching and the Santa Clause suit stank of fish. I assumed that Richie Sharp, manager of *Poundland*, had got it from his Uncle Glenn. Glenn used to work on the fish quay and, for many years, was Santa at the kids' Xmas parties at the Boilermaker's Club – until he'd got hammered one year and started telling the kids which of their mothers he'd shagged. And how.

"Yo. Ho ho," I hollered, with all the dignity of a Tibetan Monk awaiting execution. "Who has been a good boy or girl? Who wants to see Santa?" I had to shout because a dance mix of Wombling Merry Christmas was being played at full volume for the one hundredth time.

A little girl with a snotty noses came up, jumped on my knee and nearly winded me. She was just ten. Stone.

"And what's your name?" I wheezed.

"Hannah- Lee," she said, picking her nose.

"And what do you want for Christmas, Hannah – Lee?" I said.

"A Litre Bottle of Diamond Star. Me mam won't share hers with me anymore," she said, wiping snot all over my Santa suit.

A dishevelled figure stuck his head into the converted cupboard that acted as 'Santa's Ghetto' and nodded at me. I pushed Hannah-Lee away and give her a bag of cheap, Made In Taiwan tat. "Merry New Year," I growled.

I looked at the line of kids starting to head towards me and was instantly reminded of *Children Of The Corn*.

"I'll see you in King Johns in five minutes. What are you gargling?" said aka Brynn.

"A pint of wife beater," I said.

"I thought you were on the wagon, Ordy?" said Bryn.

"I'll be throwing myself under a wagon soon enough, if I don't get a drink," I said.

***

The palatial home of Sharon Kirby, now Mrs Lillian Hope, and her offspring, was a massive mock-Tudor detached house decorated in a style so chintzy that Stevie Wonder would consider it tasteless.

Nick Hope had grown into a less ugly version of his father. He was leaning over a full size snooker table and concentrating on potting a pink. I'd watched him play for the last half hour and he was good. His opponent was Vernon Reeves, a balding old booze hound who I remember being a snooker superstar when I was a kid. Nick was trouncing him.

It wasn't long before Nick cleared the table. He shook hands with Reeves and handed him a wad of cash. Reeves lit up like the Oxford Street Christmas Lights and was out of the door in a flash.

Nick walked over to a small bar in the corner of the room.

"Right, now he's gone we can have a drink. And talk shop," said Nick. He poured out two large whiskies and brought them over to the round card table where I sat.

"I assumed that you drank whisky. What with you being a private eye, and all," he said, handing me a glass. The assumptions that people make!

"Oh yes," I said, perhaps a little too enthusiastically. The best thing about stopping drinking was always starting up again.

Nick glanced at my business card, smiled and put it in the top pocket of his Ralph Loren shirt.

"So, business is going well, then," I said, looking

around the room.

"You could say that," said Nick. "Recession or not, there's always a place for snooker halls. And a few amusement arcades, too, eh?'

"I'm sure," I said. The whisky was good. A lot better than the stuff that I usually bought. I could get a taste for it if I made the right money. "The slot machines are always popular with people who have no dosh!"

"Yeah. I've a lot of them around the town. Stardust Lil's."

"Yeah, our mum runs them. Keeps her busy and up to date with the gossip."

"Is your mother around?" I said. "I think we should discuss this with her here."

Nick looked at a watch that wouldn't have looked out of place on Michael Douglas in *Wall Street*.

"Give her about five minutes. I sent her a text to tell her that you're here. She's a bit surprised. More than a bit, to be honest."

"Surprised, I'm friggindum-friggin- founded!" said a husky voice from behind me.

I looked around and saw what was possibly the shortest and definitely the most suntanned woman that I'd ever seen.

"Cocktail!" she barked and Nick leapt to his feet and headed over to the bar.

Lily Hope threw off her high heels and almost disappeared as she sank into a red leather armchair.

"So, what's the story Jackanory?" she said.

***

Another difference between the world inhabited by the silver screen private eyes and mine is the murky area of ethics and loyalty to your client. After I got back I met Tommy and gave him Sharon and Nick's address. And I took my payment with no feelings of guilt. I'd done what he'd paid me for, after all.

If I did have a twinge of remorse, however, it would have been over the fact that Lily and Nick had paid me not to tell Billy that they'd be waiting for him when he turned up. With a kitchen bench. Or two.

Ethics? Somewhere nears Suthics, I think.

Who Killed Skippy?

"Could be worse, could be raining," said Craig, pretty much as soon as it started pissing down.

A big grin crawled across his flushed face like a caterpillar. He was sniffling away and wiping his runny nose with the sleeve of his leather jacket. Craig had just snorted a sugar bowl full of Colombian marching powder and popped a veritable cornucopia of multi-coloured pills. He was talking ten to the dozen and doing my napper in no end.

I forced a smile, though I was none too pleased. I was getting soaked to the skin in a vandalised cemetery, after spending the last half hour digging a grave while Craig turned himself into a walking pharmaceutical experiment.

"Let's get on with this," I said, grabbing the dead kangaroo by its legs. But Craig was away with the fairies again, watching a flock of black birds land on a cluster of graffiti stained gravestones.

"A murder of crows," said Craig. "That's the collective noun for crows, you know? A murder."

Craig was an autodidact, hooked on learning a word a day, as well as many other things.

"Yes, Craig, I did used to be an English teacher, you know," I said. My patience was getting frayed. The rain had slipped down the back of my shirt, trickled down my spine and crept into my arse crack.

"They say that crows are harbingers of death, eh, Ordy? Have you ever wondered why they never seem to talk about harbingers of good things?"

I was now inches away from picking up the shovel and twatting Craig, but thankfully he suddenly seemed to break out of his trance. He bent down and grabbed the kangaroo.

"Let's get a move on, Ordy, eh?" he said. "It's 'Super Seventies Special' at The Grand Hotel tonight. We haven't got all day, you know?"

***

Craig was the youngest of the four Ferry boys and he'd been born premature and weak, leading his mother to become a tad overprotective of him. For most of his childhood he hardly left her side and he had, it seemed, developed a bit of an Oedipus complex. Hence, his regular attendance at the 'Super Seventies Special.' At The Grand Hotel.

Which meant that I had to go there too, since, to all intents and purposes, I was Craig's minder. Not that I was anyway near a tough guy. And not that Craig needed a bodyguard. He was well over six feet with a physique worthy of Mike Tyson.

Craig had been a sickly child, as I said, but when he reached sixteen and his mother died, he transformed himself, in a manner akin to that of Bruce Banner turning into the Incredible Hulk, albeit at a decidedly slower rate.

No, I wasn't employed by the Ferry family to protect Craig from other people. I was paid to protect him from himself.

***

I'd first met Craig when I was about twelve. We went to different comprehensive schools, so I didn't have much contact with him but I'd sometimes notice this gangling, scarecrow of a kid hanging around the local betting shop, which was owned by Glyn and Tina Ferry. He always looked lost, sat on the step reading *Commando* war comics and sipping from a bottle of *Lucozade*.

One day, during a long hot summer, bored and kicking a ball against wall, I noticed Craig and asked him if he fancied a game of football. I never would have bothered normally, you could tell by the look of him that he'd be rubbish at football, but all my friends were away at *Butlins* or *Pontins*, or some other holiday camp, and needs must.

Craig must have been bored himself, I think he'd read the ink from the stack of comics he had next to him, and he said yes.

"Okay," I'd said. "We'll do penalties. You're in goal."

Craig shuffled over to one side of the garages. One of the walls had the wobbly lined shape of a goal painted on it. He stretched his arms and legs wide.

I put the heavy leather ball on the penalty spot and stepped back for a run.

"Blow a whistle," I shouted at Craig.

"Eh?"

"A whistle,"

He pursed his lips looking more than a bit girly and I started to giggle.

"No, like this yer big girl's blouse," I said and put my fingers inside my mouth to show him. But before I could start, I heard a shriek.

I jumped, but not as much as Craig. An overweight women wearing a sleeveless, polka dot dress was running toward Craig, her bingo wings flapping.

"Get here now," she said, clasping him toward a bosom that would be accurately described as ample, before pulling him back to the betting shop.

***

It was now creeping towards the part of the night that I really hated. It was close to midnight and Craig was hammered.

"The pint of no return," he said. He downed a pint in one and staggered across the sticky carpet to the dance floor.

The Grand was crowded, hot and clammy. Billy Blockbuster, the DJ and quizmaster, was playing smoochy songs back-to-back. As *Betcha By Golly Wow* played, Craig canoodled with a couple of members of the cast of *The Golden Girls*. He could hardly stand up, and the pensioners were doing all that they could to support him, but it wouldn't be long before Goliath would crash down.

And, before you could shout 'Timber!' he was over, crushing one of the women beneath him. Two bouncers in Crombies, Darren and Dane Greenwood, ran over but when they saw it was Craig they just stepped back and looked at me.

You could hear the screams of the old woman trapped beneath Craig so Billy Blockbuster quickly changed the song to The Jam's *Going Underground* and pumped up the volume.

"Well?" said Dane.

"Aye," I said.

Darren went back to the door and Dane bent down and grabbed Craig's ankles while I took hold of him by his, frankly minging, armpits.

He was a dead weight as we dragged him up, just enough so someone could pull the woman from underneath him. We struggled and turned him on his back. He was in a deep sleep, snogging with Morpheus and snoring like a hammer drill.

And then it was the hard part.

***

Craig's father, Glyn Ferry, was a terrifying man by reputation although he was rarely seen in action. His foot soldiers were his boys. Alanby, William and Dafydd. William did most of the muscle work while Dafydd did the greasing of palms and the like. And Alanby, well, he was known as The Enforcer and he was in prison for murder for most of my childhood but, one day when I was about thirteen, he got out.

I'd just finished my supper, spread cheese on toast, and was sitting with my mam watching Callan. My dad was on night shift at the Lighthouse and the house was calm until there was a rapid knock at the door. My mother, ever stoic and unruffled, slowly got to her feet and, keeping an eye on the television, looked out of the window,

"By the cringe!" she said. This was as much as she swore. "What does he want at this time of night?"

Callan and Lonely were arguing on TV and I wasn't really paying attention to her but I looked up when she came back from the door with Craig who was white and shaking.

"It's Wednesday," I said, angrily. "Comic club is Thursday nights." It had been a tradition over the last few years that every Thursday, Craig and a couple of other waifs and strays came to my house and we swapped comics.

"It's our Alanby," stuttered Craig.

"What?" I said. My mother was giving him a sympathetic look, which was grating on me. There were another twenty minutes of Callan left.

"Why not sit down, luvvie," said my mother. "I'll make you a cup of sweet tea and you can tell us all about it."

She pushed Craig down into dad's armchair and went into the kitchen. I turned my attention to the TV until the adverts came on.

Mam gave Craig his tea in a Seatown F.C. mug and he took sips, making annoying slurping noises.

The story that stumbled out of Craig, in fits and starts, was that Alanby had been released from jail after ten years inside. And he'd come home with a bride, Trish, a Scottish prostitute he'd met two days after getting out.

Craig's parents were none too pleased and had

kicked them out of their home shortly after they arrived. So, Alanby and Trish moved into a flat above one of the betting shops. Short of cash, and with a big heroin habit, Alanby had put Trish back on the game.

That night, she'd picked up a Dutch sailor down at the docks and sold him her wedding ring in The Shipp Inn. Alanby had turned up at the pub in a drunken rage and sliced Trish to pieces. He'd then turned up at his parents' home covered in blood and wanting a change of clothes. Craig had opened the door to the blood splattered Alanby and had freaked out.

He spent the next few nights staying at my house, working his way through my mam's *Readers Digests* and the Ferry's got into the habit of packing him off to stay with me whenever they wanted him out of the way.

Well, at least these days they paid.

***

I'd never put much stock in all that hereditary cobblers. Bad blood and the like. I was more of a nurture over nature man. Though it did seem to me that The Ferry family were all born under a bad star.

Except Beverly, that is. Beverly was the only girl of the Ferry siblings. She was a qualified accountant who did the firm's books and worked in the local civic centre. And her business acumen was a real boon to the family, especially when their enterprises became more and more legit. And she was the one that had decided to hire me to keep a bleary eye on Craig.

Beverly was in her late thirties. She was well read. She was good looking. She was fun to be with. And I had been arse over tit in love with her for as long as I could remember. And, of course, she was married. To a local

Councillor, to boot.

I'd managed to manoeuvre Craig in and out of the taxi and through the front door of his flat but was having trouble getting him up the stairs. I was still aching from all that digging I'd done and was considering giving up the ghost, and leaving Craig where he lay, when his mobile started to ring.

I took it out of his pocket and looked at the display. It was Beverly. I switched off the *Bonanza* theme and spoke.

"Craig's phone, Peter Ord, speaking."

"Oh, God, is he trashed again, Peter?"

"Either that or he's rehearsing for his *Stars In Your Eyes* appearance as Oliver Reed."

A chuckle.

"Alright, I suppose I'll see him tomorrow," she said. "It was just that he had a delivery job to do earlier and I wanted to make sure it had gone well. Know anything about it?"

"Er … yeah, I think …"

"Shit, he bolloxed it up, didn't he?"

"Well …"

"Peter, I can tell when you're telling pork pies. I'll be there in bit."

***

Bev was looking very business-like in a sharp black suit and high heels, her blonde hair tied back. And she looked more than somewhat pissed off.

"So, who was the idiot with the Luger?" she said. She had to raise her voice slightly as Craig's snores were now echoing through the living room. We'd managed to get him on the sofa and left him there. We moved into the cramped kitchen and I took a can of *Fosters* from the fridge.

"Fancy one?"

Bev shook her head.

"So, the Shogun Assassin?"

"Dunno who he was. Craig said that the bloke pissed off on a motorbike before he could get his hands on him. Was dressed head to foot in black, like a ninja, apparently."

"Yeah, well our Craig has always been blessed with an over ripe imagination."

"True, true."

"A ninja with a Luger sounds like something from one of those comics you two used to read. Was he on anything?"

"Yeah, a motorbike," I said

"Not the ninja, you plonker, Craig!"

"Ah, well…"

"Jesus. I thought you were supposed to keep an eye on him?"

"Hey, he was already as high as Sly by the time I met him."

The story was this: One of the Ferry family's occasional entrepreneurial activities was importing unusual animals through the docks and selling them to collectors of exotic pets. One such collector was Bobby Bowles, the former football superstar, who had a private zoo just outside Seatown.

Craig's job was to deliver a kangaroo to Bobby in exchange for a wad of dosh. However, on his way to Bowles' place, Craig's van was stopped by a ninja with a gun who shot the kangaroo and scarped on a Harley Davidson. Craig phoned me to help him get rid of Skippy's body, of course, hence my fun day at the graveyard.

"This is a very bloody important time for the family business," said Bev. "Dad's very ill, Alanby is never going to get out of Wakefield nick since he spiked that warden's tea with ecstasy and Dafydd is, well, Dafydd …"

Dafydd had, for many years, been so far in the closet he was in Narnia but when he eventually came out he shocked the family by moving down south to open up a scuba diving club with an Australian. This was blamed for causing Glyn Ferry's first heart attack.

"So, Craig is being groomed to take over as head of the family business?" I said.

Bev raised her eyebrows.

"Supposedly," she said.

"Oh, dear," I said.

"Oh, dear, indeed," said Bev.

***

We were sitting in 'Velvettes Gentleman's Club' staring behind the bar at a stained glass recreation of the famed poster of the female tennis player scratching her arse.

"Lesbians?" I said. I finished my pint of *Stella*. I was well and truly off the wagon now.

"Yep," said Craig.

"I've never heard that one before."

"Aye. Good With Colours is a euphemism for gay men and Tennis Fans is for lesbians."

"Well, as always, Craig, you are an education."

"Well, you should read more, shouldn't you? Might learn something."

I finished my drink and went over to the bar. The dancers were starting to arrive at Velvettes. It was a couple of hours before opening time but Jack Martin, the owner, usually gave them a little booze up on a Saturday night to get them in the mood. Jack was more of your benevolent kind of gangster.

"But I think you're avoiding the issue, Craig," I said, as I sat back down. "What are you going to do now?"

"Well, I'll see if Jack needs anyone for a bit of occasional strong-arm work. Him and dad are on good terms. For the moment, anyway."

"But Bev's the family gaffer now?"

"Yep, pretty much. Head of the family. The God-sister. Dad's said he can't trust me after 'The Kangaroo Incident', as he calls it."

"You ever find out who shot Skippy? Or why?"

"Not a clue. And Bev doesn't seem too bothered about finding them, either. Thinks they were from out of town. Albania or somewhere. She thinks we might have been encroaching on their territory."

"Oh, can't go around encroaching. Well out of order, that."

As the girls hovered around the bar there was a cacophony of foreign accents. It was nice. A welcome change.

Contact with foreigners was once, in fact, such a rarity that, legend had it, during the Napoleonic wars the people of Seatown had hanged a monkey because they thought it was a French spy. Not an unreasonable mistake, in many people's minds. So, I suppose you could say that there was a track record of exotic animals coming to an unfortunate end in Seatown.

It was also very hard to keep a secret here.

Which was why I knew all about Bev's new Harley Davidson, even if the rest of her family didn't. And why I wasn't particularly shocked when she'd mentioned Craig's attacker using a Luger, even though I hadn't mentioned it to her before.

I did consider sharing this information with Craig, of course. Well, for all of five minutes, I did.

It was pretty clear that the Ferry family were in safe hands with Bev ruling the roost. And it was certainly a lot safer for me to have her on my side than against me. After all, despite what Craig may have thought, it wasn't what you knew that mattered in life, it was who you knew.

The Lady & The Gimp

They say that it never rains, but it pours, and that troubles are like buses – they all turn up at once. They say a lot of things, though. And most of what they say is about as much use as a condom in a convent.

For example, they also say that lightning never strikes twice. Which is a pretty clear indication, to my mind, that 'they' had never encountered Lightning Jones.

Lightning was very tall, very beautiful and very loud.

Very, very loud. Her voice boomed around the room and her laugh had such timbre and volume that she could have started an avalanche if she were near a mountain.

As it was, we were in Harry Shand's Bar. Earlier that day, I'd had a phone call from my old school friend, Barry Blue. Barry was working at Shand's tonight and he had a job for me. I jumped at the chance. I'd just finished a missing person's case which involved an errant husband who I'd found living above a dirty book shop in Walton Street with a girl a little younger than his daughter. Pretty much standard stuff and, unfortunately, standard pay. I needed to earn a bit more than that, though. I owed three weeks rent and the landlord was losing patience. Carl 'Rachman' Raymond wasn't particularly renowned for his patience, either.

Barry was in the corner of the room repairing the antique Wurlitzer Jukebox which Shand had bought from the Krugers after they closed down the '50s style American diner.

It took him less than five minutes to fix it. He was good with machines. But women were another story, however.

"Fixed?" said Lightning as she loomed over Barry.

Barry blushed and stuttered an affirmative.

Women usually did that to him, which was probably why he still lived with his mother even though he was well past his sell-by date. And Lightning Jones was some kind of a woman. She was tall with long black hair, a ripped black t-shirt, high heels, leather skirt and fishnet stockings. And she looked like she was literally taking Barry's breath away.

"Thanks, luv," she said with a muddy, drunken slur. She leaned over and gave Barry a peck on the cheek. Barry was so embarrassed that he looked like Vesuvius waiting to erupt. He rushed over to the bar and sat next to me, still burning up. Shand walked over and patted him on the back

"Thanks youngster," said Shand, handing Barry a brown envelope.

"Any time, Uncle Shandy," said Barry, a tremor in his voice.

"What can I get you boys?" asked Shand. Shand had big bushy eyebrows almost meeting in the middle which made him look constantly confused.

"IrnBru, please," said Barry with a slight lisp.

The massive barman, whose name tag said 'Titch', poured an IrnBru for Barry and a beer for me.

The *'Bonanza Theme'* blasted out of the jukebox and Lightning screeched and danced around the room like a wild woman. From flamenco to tango in less than five minutes. And back again.

"She's amazing!" gasped Barry.

"She is, indeed," I said. "Clearly a can short of a six pack but amazing, nevertheless."

"She looks familiar," I said to Titch.

"Liz Jones," said Titch. "She used to be the singer in that punk band Pulp Metal before they moved down to the smoke. They called her Lightning because she used to swig from a two litre bottle of White Lightning onstage."

"I remember," I said. "Wasn't she a blonde?"

"Yeah," said Titch. "But the collars and cuffs didn't match."

"She's amazing," said Barry, again, looking a bit on the mesmerized side.

"Best keep away from her, lads." said Titch, giving us our drinks. "She's got issues."

"Let he who is without sin," I said. "We've all got our issues you know?" I sipped my pint and raised it to him in a mock toast.

"Yeah," said the barman. "But her issues are about

six-foot-six with a psychotically violent temper and are currently doing time in Durham nick for a string of horrible murders. You've heard of Spammy Spampinato, haven't you?"

"The bloke who burnt down Jack Martin's strip joint?"

Titch nodded and Barry and I shuffled off to sit in the corner, Barry looking a little crestfallen.

"Do you come here often?" Barry said, with a grin. I was keeping an eye on Lightning who was now dancing on a table and looking to be in danger of doing herself a mischief.

"Not if I can help it," I said. "I feel about as welcome as a wino in a Wine Bar."

"Not really my cup of tea, either," said Barry. "I do go to the Indoor Bowls Club in Charleston Road every now and then, though. I like the quiz. Or I did."

In lots of ways, Barry hadn't changed. He was middle aged now, like me, but he was still baby faced and still wore a waxy, blue raincoat and thick framed glasses with lenses that looked like jam-jar bottoms. And still a mine of useless information who really came to life during pub quizzes.

"So, what's the story?" I said. "How's Mrs. Blue?"

Barry gazed over at Lightning who was doing a Can-Can on the Bar. Titch was ignoring her, reading a well-thumbed copy of Colin Wilson's *The Outsider*.

"She's scarpered," said Barry.

"What?" I said.

"Yeah, she's done a runner with Mike Evers, the ginger Welsh bloke that did the quiz in the Bowls Club. Ginger, mind you!"

Barry had a thing about red headed people. It went back to our schooldays. Like most kids he had a few nicknames at school: Barry Poo, Barry Spew, that sort of thing, but the one that stuck was 'The Gimp.'

Ron Penhaligon was the PE teacher that had christened him 'The Gimp'. Penhaligon was short and stocky with freckles and bright red hair. He had glasses as thick as Barry's and his shoulders had more chips than Harry Ramsden. He found particular amusement in tormenting those unfortunates who turned up for PE without their kit, or with sick notes. And, for whatever sadistic reason, the rotten apple of Penhaligon's bleary eye was Barry. He jumped at any opportunity he could to bring out 'The Gimp' and humiliate him in front of the rest of the class.

There were more than a few of us who gleaned a fair bit of satisfaction when Penhaligon was sent down for playing hide the salami with an under aged student.

"So what are you doing then? Living on your todd?" I said.

"Aye," said Barry. "Still got the house, though. Dad left it to me, not Ma so ..."

Lightning jumped off the bar and came over to us. She picked up a box of matches and lit a black French cigarette. She blew a chain of smoke rings.

"Yeah," said Barry, looking uncomfortable. "It's a bit weird living in that big four bedroom place all by myself."

Lightning's eyes seemed to flicker and I'm quite sure I saw her pupils become pound signs. The French version of Jane Morgan's *The Day The Rains Came* was the next song up. Lightning started to sway to the music, in her own world. She blew Barry a kiss and went back to the bar.

"So, I take it you want me to find your mother, then?" I said.

Barry nodded.

"I never trusted that Ginger twat, mind you. I reckon he knows about the Ma's little nest egg, her pension fund, and he's fleecing her."

"So, you think they've gone to Wales? I've never been abroad before. Will I need a passport?"

"I doubt it. I heard that he's got a wife and kids back there, grandkids even. This is why he ended up here."

"So where's he been staying?"

I noticed that Lightning and Titch were deep in conversation, occasionally glancing over at us. My spider senses startled tingling. Well, it was either that or eczema.

"Apparently, the last few years he's been living at a rooming house in Eastside. It's run by this old Polish woman. Her husband was a pilot in the Battle Of Britain. She doesn't seem to speak much English, though. She wouldn't tell me anything, anyway."

"Okay, I'll go over there with Big Mark Nowak and see if he can get anything out of her. What do you want me to do when I see your mum?"

"Nothing," said Barry. "Just tell me where she is and I'll speak to her."

I nodded.

"I'll double your fee if you find her before the end of the month. Her pension goes in the bank then."

"Okay, suits me sir! I'm off over home," I said, standing up. 'Want to share a taxi? I can drop you off at Charleston Road?"

"No. No," said Barry. "I'll stay here a bit longer. See if the jukebox conks out, like. You never know. Tricky things these antiques."

His eyes were on Lightning as he spoke to me and she had the look of a black widow spider about her. A decidedly peckish one at that.

***

Lightning was sitting on a table close to the bar and was canoodling on Barry's lap. They'd been like that all night. And Barry, for the first time since I'd known him, was as drunk as a skunk.

The jukebox was kicking out Howling Wolf's *I Ain't Superstitious* and Barry was, after a fashion, attempting to sing along. Strange though it may seem, this was the happiest that I'd ever seen him.

"So, your Welsh friend left his last digs last week without paying his rent. Did a runner with two weeks due," I said.

Barry was oblivious to me as he snuggled up to Lightning but she was giving me her complete attention.

"And do you know where Mrs Blue is?" she said.

I shrugged.

"Well, Mrs Kapuszinska, using her more earthly contacts – gossips from the bingo – thinks he's staying in a caravan up at Happy Valley. I'll go over and check it out tomorrow morning."

I glanced at Barry who was asleep with his head in Lightning's cleavage.

"I'll phone Barry when I know for certain the Welshman's there. Maybe after mid-day? Give him a chance to sleep it off?"

"Better leave it until well after mid-day. We'll be busy."

"Yeah?"

"Yeah, we're getting married in the morning. Just like the song," she said, grinning like a game show host.

***

I pulled up Mrs Blue sitting on the step of a caravan, smoking and reading a copy of Hello magazine.

"Mrs Blue, it's Peter. Peter Ord. Barry's mate from school."

"I remember you," she said, squinting. "You used to collect them American comics with drawings of muscle men in them. We had you down as a shirt-lifter."

I grimaced.

"Nice to see you again, too," I said. Though it had rarely been nice to see Mrs Blue.

***

It was usually about the time when he saw Mrs Blue with her ear pressed to a glass that she'd put against the wall that Barry knew he'd be moving home again, soon.

It was the regular pattern throughout his childhood. He and his parents would move into a flat above a shop or a terraced house or some other type of private rented accommodation. And things would be fine and Jim Dandy for a while. But somewhere along the way, Mrs Blue would start to get jealous. She'd be suspicious of her husband's comings and goings. Well, mostly his comings. She'd usually suspect one of the neighbours or a woman from the corner shop. She'd ask Mr Blue where he'd been when he'd come in from work, even though he was covered in crap from working shifts in the foundry. This would escalate into a screaming match, with plates and cups smashed against the wall.

Then Mrs Blue would start spying. She'd keep Barry off school so he could walk the streets with her looking for Mr Blue and 'fallen women'. When it got really bad she'd call the police and say that her husband's fancy women were trying to burn the house down. Or there'd be a fight with someone she'd accused of making the two backed beast with her husband. And so she'd be sectioned again and given the old EST. Then she'd come out of hospital and they'd move home and everything would be okay until it started again.

When Mr Blue died of asbestosis, Barry and his mother were left with a massive wad of insurance and compensation money. So, Barry gave up his job at the Thermos flask factory to take care of his sick Ma.

She didn't look that sick now though. She was dolled up to the nines, wearing a red PVC dress and a leopard skin coat. It seemed as if it had done her and Barry the world of good when she'd moved out.

"Did our Barry send you to look for me?" she said.

"Aye."

"Does he know where I am?"

"Not yet."

"Are you going to tell him, then?" she said.

"That's my job, Mrs Blue. I'm a private eye now," I said.

She finished her cigarette, put it out, and lit up another one in a flash.

"How's he doing?"

I took out a bottle of water and glugged it down in one.

"Not too bad," I said. "In fact, he's getting married later today."

She started to laugh.

"Yeah?"

"Yeah, really," I said.

"He told you tell me that didn't he? To get me to come back."

"Naw, it's true!"

Mrs Blue made a tutting sound, stood up and

walked back into the caravan.

"Piss off back to your comics, son," she said, as she slammed the door.

***

The turnout at Barry and Lightning's wedding wasn't exactly of Charles and Diana standard, apparently. It wasn't even Charles and Camilla standard. Just Harry Shand and a couple of booze hounds. But the low attendance was more than compensated for by the appearance of Mrs Blue bursting into the registry office brandishing a golf club and screaming at Lightning, calling her a number of variations of the word slut.

This resulted in Lightning giving Mrs Blue a gut punch which had her doubled over and puking. Barry then grabbed Lightning by the throat and continued Mrs Blue's dialogue theme as he tried to throttle her. And then Lightning turned to Barry and punched him in the jaw, knocking him clean out. Which was what I meant by Lightning striking twice.

Not that I saw any of this, of course. I was feeling a tad delicate after my meeting with Mrs Blue so I decided to go back home and have a kip before phoning Barry and telling him of his mother's whereabouts.

Not the best idea, in retrospect.

***

The evening was melting into night and dark, malignant clouds were spreading themselves across the sky. I pulled down the metal shutters and locked up Las Vegas Amusements as a battered yellow taxi cab spluttered to a halt in front of the arcade. Living above an amusement arcade was hardly ideal but my landlord, Mr Raymond, give me a cheap deal as long as I locked up the place and did the bingo when one of the callers rang in sick.

I shuffled into the back seat and was attacked by the overpowering aroma of air freshener and blow.

"Where to?" said the taxi driver, a constipated looking rat boy with a checked Burberry baseball cap and a crackly shell suit.

"Belle Vue Cemetery," I said.

"Dead centre of town, eh?" said the driver as the taxi coughed itself to life.

In less than ten minutes, we were outside the Belle Vue Cemetery's wrought iron gates. I paid the driver and popped into *Costcutter* for a can of wife beater to get me through the morning and a bunch of flowers. I downed half of it as I stood at the counter. The tall Sikh that served me paid me no heed as I pushed the can into my jacket pocket,

As I rushed into the graveyard I bumped into the gangling form of Reverend Abbott, pulling up his fly as his stepped out of a Portaloo. He nodded and we walked toward the grave together.

Mrs Blue was inconsolable although the big ginger Welshman next to her was doing his best. Harry Shand, complete with a black eye and an arm in a sling stood scowling. Then, Reverend Abbott, his long hair flowing in the cold north wind began his eulogy.

"There comes a time in every young man's life,' he said, his long arms stretched wide. 'When he knows that he will never be The Fonz ...'

I tuned out after that. It was clear where he was going, though. Poor Barry wasn't one of life's lucky ones.

A couple of days after he split up from Lightning and his mother moved back in with him, there was knock at the door. Spammy Spampinato's brother, Little Joey, was standing there with a baseball bat which he proceeded to use to redecorate the Blue household. Harry Shand, who was visiting, tried to intervene but it was no use. Little Joey Spampinato was only known as 'Little' due to his age rather than his size. And once again Barry got in the way. He was dead before he got to the hospital.

Abbott finished his rambling eulogy and we all threw dirt and flowers on the coffin.

"Do you want to say something Peter?" said Shand, as rain began to pour down in sheets.

I shuffled around and then took the half empty can of Stella from my jacket pocket.

"Here's to Barry Blue," I said. "Unlucky in love and not much cop at cards, either.

48379781R00061

Printed in Poland
by Amazon Fulfillment
Poland Sp. z o.o., Wrocław